Bonn ... ooped
over and picked up her nightclothes and slipped them
back on.

"Maybe, in town . . ." she said to Slocum.

"Maybe," he said. He began to put on his black pants
and shirt. He pulled on his boots as Bonnie walked back
to the wagon.

Slocum sat down and waited until it was quiet again.
Then he plucked a cheroot from his pocket, lit it with a
lucifer, and smoked.

Halfway through his cigar, he heard a muffled sound. Instinctively, he reached for his gun belt and unwrapped it.

He peered into the darkness in the direction of the soft
sound.

His hand slid to the handle of his bowie knife. He saw
a silver flash in the moonlight.

One shadow in the night grew larger and started toward him.

Slocum drew his knife and stubbed out his cheroot.

The shadow crept closer and he saw the form of a man
and the man held a blade in his hand.

Slocum lay flat and the shadow began to run toward him.

Ten feet away, he saw the Apache, silent as a cat, running toward him at full speed, running toward the hobbled
horses.

When the Apache was two yards away, Slocum rose up.
He held the big blade at his waist, ready to strike.

DON'T MISS THESE
ALL-ACTION WESTERN SERIES
FROM THE BERKLEY PUBLISHING GROUP

THE GUNSMITH by J. R. Roberts

Clint Adams was a legend among lawmen, outlaws, and ladies. They called him . . . the Gunsmith.

LONGARM by Tabor Evans

The popular long-running series about Deputy U.S. Marshal Custis Long—his life, his loves, his fight for justice.

SLOCUM by Jake Logan

Today's longest-running action Western. John Slocum rides a deadly trail of hot blood and cold steel.

BUSHWHACKERS by B. J. Lanagan

An action-packed series by the creators of Longarm! The rousing adventures of the most brutal gang of cutthroats ever assembled—Quantrill's Raiders.

DIAMONDBACK by Guy Brewer

Dex Yancey is Diamondback, a Southern gentleman turned con man when his brother cheats him out of the family fortune. Ladies love him. Gamblers hate him. But nobody pulls one over on Dex . . .

WILDGUN by Jack Hanson

The blazing adventures of mountain man Will Barlow—from the creators of Longarm!

TEXAS TRACKER by Tom Calhoun

J.T. Law: the most relentless—and dangerous—manhunter in all Texas. Where sheriffs and posses fail, he's the best man to bring in the most vicious outlaws—for a price.

JAKE LOGAN

SLOCUM
AND THE GLITTER
GIRLS AT GRAVEL GULCH

JOVE BOOKS, NEW YORK

THE BERKLEY PUBLISHING GROUP
Published by the Penguin Group
Penguin Group (USA) Inc.
375 Hudson Street, New York, New York 10014, USA
Penguin Group (Canada), 90 Eglinton Avenue East, Suite 700, Toronto, Ontario M4P 2Y3, Canada
(a division of Pearson Penguin Canada Inc.) • Penguin Books Ltd., 80 Strand, London WC2R 0RL,
England • Penguin Group Ireland, 25 St. Stephen's Green, Dublin 2, Ireland (a division of Penguin
Books Ltd.) • Penguin Group (Australia), 707 Collins Street, Melbourne, Victoria 3008, Australia
(a division of Pearson Australia Group Pty. Ltd.) • Penguin Books India Pvt. Ltd., 11 Community
Centre, Panchsheel Park, New Delhi—110 017, India • Penguin Group (NZ), 67 Apollo Drive,
Rosedale, Auckland 0632, New Zealand (a division of Pearson New Zealand Ltd.) • Penguin Books
(South Africa) (Pty.) Ltd., Rosebank Office Park, 181 Jan Smuts Avenue, Parktown North 2193,
South Africa • Penguin China, B7 Jiaming Center, 27 East Third Ring Road North,
Chaoyang District, Beijing 100020, China

Penguin Books Ltd., Registered Offices: 80 Strand, London WC2R 0RL, England

This is a work of fiction. Names, characters, places, and incidents either are the product of the
author's imagination or are used fictitiously, and any resemblance to actual persons, living or
dead, business establishments, events, or locales is entirely coincidental.

SLOCUM AND THE GLITTER GIRLS AT GRAVEL GULCH

A Jove Book / published by arrangement with the author

PUBLISHING HISTORY
Jove edition / March 2013

Copyright © 2013 by Penguin Group (USA) Inc.
Cover illustration by Sergio Giovine.

ISBN: 978-0-515-15311-8

JOVE®
Jove Books are published by The Berkley Publishing Group,
a division of Penguin Group (USA) Inc.,
375 Hudson Street, New York, New York 10014.
JOVE® is a registered trademark of Penguin Group (USA) Inc.
The "J" design is a trademark of Penguin Group (USA) Inc.

PRINTED IN THE UNITED STATES OF AMERICA

10 9 8 7 6 5 4 3 2 1

ALWAYS LEARNING   **PEARSON**

1

John Slocum galloped his black horse off the small butte like roaring thunder. Ferro's hooves, newly shod in iron by a Laramie blacksmith, struck sparks from the rocks and kicked up twin spools that followed them down like rust-infused dragon's tails. He passed the four horses ground-tied to clumps of sagebrush and put the blunt spurs into Ferro's flanks with a practiced tick that parted hide and tapped into flesh. The horse stretched its neck and flattened its ears on the level road with the wind in its teeth, its tail flowing behind it like tassels of black silk.

Ahead of him was a rickety covered wagon pulled by a four-horse team, hell-bent for leather, the driver whipping the horses as he leaned out and looked back at five young Apache braves yelping their war cries and firing single-shot Sharps carbines as fast as they could load them. A man Slocum could not see, who had been sitting beside the driver, stood up with his arms outstretched and fell from the wagon. The Apache shrieks rose to a higher intensity.

Slocum saw puffs of white smoke rising from the top of

a butte off to his right. He knew that the smoke could be seen for miles. While he could not decipher the message in the small smoke puffs, he reasoned that the signals could be a summons to others of the tribe at various locations.

Two of the Apache braves turned their ponies and galloped over to the fallen man. One of them dismounted and was pulling on the downed man's hair after knocking his hat off with a single swipe of his hand.

Slocum slipped his Winchester from its sheath and let his single-looped rein fall behind the saddle horn. He cocked the rifle and heard the mechanism slide a cartridge into the firing chamber. He leveled the rifle with his right hand and braced the butt against the hollow where his shoulder joined his chest. Still, the blued barrel jumped up and down and was hard to steady. When the barrel dropped and blotted out the brave on the ground, he held his breath and squeezed the trigger. The Apache brandished a knife. Its blade glistened silver in the sun.

He levered another cartridge into the chamber and heard the ping of the empty hull striking the ground. The other brave looked at him and brought a Spencer carbine to his shoulder. He fired at Slocum. There was a puff of white smoke and a stream of orange and golden sparks that issued from the barrel.

Slocum turned his horse with knee pressure and headed for the mounted Apache.

He heard the whispery rasping sizzle of lead blow past his head with the ferocity of an angry hornet.

The Apache brave hunched low over his pony's back and the horse galloped in a zigzag motion so that Slocum could not get a clear shot. In seconds, the pony and rider were out of range, headed for the butte, where the smoke signals were no longer visible.

As Slocum approached the wagon, it slowed until it came to a full stop.

"Howdy," the driver said as he set the brake and looked back. "I'm mighty grateful you run off them redskins, stranger."

"Your shotgun is dead," Slocum said as he pulled up alongside the driver.

"I figgered that." Obadiah Gump lifted his gray felt hat, which had all but lost its shape, and wiped a bandanna across his sweat-sleek forehead. "Tom warn't with me long, but he should have had more sense than to show himself. We was outnumbered."

Slocum heard voices from inside the wagon. Terrified women's voices, voices that whispered in breathy tones.

"What have you got in there, mice?" Slocum asked.

Gump laughed.

"Got me two brides from Denver. Catalog brides, I calls 'em. They put their pictures in a paper and try to get some poor old sodbuster or miner to marry 'em."

"Mail-order brides," Slocum said.

"I calls 'em catalog brides. Most of 'em wind up takin' care of some cripple or workin' like a slave in a store or on a farm."

"Where are you headed?" Slocum asked.

"Deadfall. It's a—"

"That's where I'm going."

"You want to ride shotgun for me after I load poor Tom in the wagon?"

"I'm driving four horses there."

"Hell, tie 'em to the wagon, yours, too, and I'll pay you two dollars to ride shotgun."

Two small faces appeared behind Gump. The women wore bonnets, but were young and pretty.

"Gals, meet your rescuer. I didn't get your name, stranger."

"It's Slocum, John Slocum."

"This here's Bonnie Loomis, the one wearin' the pink

bonnet, and the other'n is Renata Simpson, under the blue bonnet."

The girls giggled. Slocum thought they couldn't have been more than nineteen or twenty. He touched a finger to his hat and nodded at them.

"Gals, we got to pick up Tom Nixon, then this gentleman's goin' to hitch up some horses to the back of the wagon and ride shotgun the rest of the way."

The two girls giggled and batted their eyes at Slocum.

He turned his horse and rode back to where Tom's body lay. The wagon rumbled up and Obie set the brake. He stepped down and Slocum slid from his saddle.

"Move up front, girls," Obie said as he dropped the tailgate.

He picked up Tom's body by the boots while Slocum lifted him from the shoulders. They slid the body onto the wagon bed. The girls were breathing hard and cringed when the dead man's head slid between them. But they did not cry out or say anything. They both jumped when Obie slammed the tailgate shut and slid the bolts to lock it in place.

"I'll wait here while you fetch your horses, Mr. Slocum," Obie said.

"Call me John. I won't be long."

"You can call me Obie, feller."

Slocum rode off to where he had left the horses. He returned in less than ten minutes. He and Obie hitched the lead rope to a wagon post, and he slid a rope around Ferro's muzzle and tied it to a post on the opposite side. He slipped his rifle from its scabbard and walked to the front of the wagon and climbed up in the seat while Obie hauled himself up into the driver's seat.

Obie clicked his teeth and rattled the reins across the backs of the four horses and turned the wagon.

Slocum looked all around on both sides of the road but saw no Apaches.

The two girls poked their heads out between Slocum and Obie.

"You going to Deadfall, too, mister?" Bonnie asked.

"I am," he said.

"We've never been there," Renata said. "What's it like?"

"I've never been there either," Slocum said.

"Ain't much of a town," Obie said. "But they struck gold in Gravel Gulch, so them boys are puttin' up shacks all over the canyon. Who you bringin' the horses to, John?"

"Man named Orson Canby bought them," Slocum said. "Know him?"

"Sure. He's a hard-rock miner who's haulin' timber from the mountains and buildin' roads all over the valley."

"I'm going to get hitched to a Mr. Wallace Hornaday," Bonnie said.

"And my groom is to be Mr. Harlan Devlin," Renata said. Then both women sighed.

Slocum looked at Obie's face. It had gone pasty, as if the blood had drained from it like egg from a broken shell. But he did not say anything. Slocum sensed that he didn't want to comment in front of the women.

"Where did you two come from?" Slocum asked.

"Fort Delaware," Bonnie said. "We took the stage to Saint Johns and that's where Obie came to meet us. This is all very exciting to us."

"We got to Fort Delaware from Denver," Renata said, "but the men we were to marry got transferred, so we advertised in the *Bride Bulletin* and both got letters from men in Deadfall. I think they're both rich."

"We hope so. All we saw in Denver were derelicts and gamblers. And Fort Delaware was like being in a prison behind the high walls of the stockade."

"They's been a few women what have come to Deadfall," Obie said. "Don't know if any of 'em got married, though. Some was workin' at the Wild Horse Saloon or took on washerwoman jobs. But that was a while ago. Town's growed since then."

"Why is it called Deadfall?" Slocum asked.

"The prospector who rode into that great big old valley a-huntin' deer or antelope come across a gulch where somebody had camped. There were all kinds of traps and several deadfalls, a little cabin. Man inside the cabin was a skeleton by then, starved to death or kilt by a b'ar, but he had a sack of gold and the feller who found him also found a map and stakes along the creek. There was the skeletons of animals under some of the deadfalls, so he started callin' the place Deadfall. He hired help out of Flagstaff and then somebody kilt him and took over his claim. But by that time, news of the strike had got out and the valley began to fill up with miners and all sorts of people who make their money off of prospectors."

"A boomtown," Slocum said as the wagon rumbled along the dirt road toward low mountains and timber.

"Kind of," Obie said.

"I just love gold things," Renata said. "Bracelets and earrings, gold wedding rings."

"Me, too," Bonnie said. "My groom said he had lots of gold."

"Oh, there's gold there, all right," Obie said. "And along with it, plenty of sin and skullduggery, like any boomtown."

Slocum rocked in the seat, his rifle across his lap. He pulled a cheroot from his pocket, slid a matchbox out of another pocket, and bit off the end of the cigar. Then he lit the cheroot.

He didn't know what awaited the girls in Deadfall, but he'd seen a lot of mail-order brides wind up in brothels or gambling houses, lured to Western towns with the promise of marriage and then finding that all that glittered was not gold.

He began to form a picture of Deadfall in his mind, and thought he knew why Obie had blanched when he heard the names of the men who had sent for the women.

The women were young and pretty, and one of them, Renata, was stroking his arm with a single finger.

He felt as if he were being petted, like a dog or a cat.

Deadfall was still more than a half day away by his reckoning, and he knew they would not make it to the valley by nightfall.

Meanwhile, there were two young women in season and likely they had waited some time for male companionship.

Anything, or almost anything, could happen in that desolate, sun-baked country where the towering buttes shone like painted castles in the afternoon sun.

2

The falling sun glistened on the buttes and on the dark sides of them, the shadows stretching eastward in long carpets. There was a sudden chill to the breeze, and as the wagon approached the fringe of the low tree-flocked hills, they heard something crack beneath the wagon. The wagon tilted crazily before Obie reined the team to a halt.

"What was that?" Slocum asked.

Obie set the brake.

"Sounded like we broke a spoke."

"Or maybe two," Slocum said.

Both men climbed down from the seat and walked around the wagon. One wheel was canted away from the wagon, tilted at a crazy angle.

"Spokes broke all right," Obie said. "Lucky I got some spares in the toolbox."

"Take long to fix them?" Slocum asked.

"Have to jack up the wagon, take off the wheel, slip out them three broke spokes, and fit three new ones." Obie looked up at the western sky, the shadows welling up in the hills. The breeze cooled the sweat on his face and dried it to a filmy transparent paste. He wiped his face with his sodden bandanna.

"We'll have to camp right here, I reckon," Obie said. "Be full dark before I'm finished."

"I'll help all I can," Slocum said.

"Just keep your eyes peeled for any more 'Paches."

"It's some quiet out here now," Slocum said as he surveyed the empty landscape. "Maybe too damned quiet."

"Just keep that rifle of your'n handy," Obie said.

The two women peered out of the wagon, their faces just above the tailgate.

"I felt a lurch," Renata said. "What happened?"

"Busted wheel," Obie said. "You gals can crawl out of there and stretch your legs. Don't go far."

"How long do we have to stay here?" Bonnie asked as Renata lifted one leg over the tailgate and prepared to let herself out of the wagon and onto the ground.

"We'll spend the night here," Obie said. "You gals can sleep in the wagon if you don't mind the smell of Tom. I'll spread my blankets underneath the wagon."

Slocum looked at the horses. "I'll lay my bedroll where I can keep an eye on the horses and the wagon," he said.

"You gals can start lookin' for some stones to put in a circle to make a fire ring, and see if you can't rustle up something to burn so's we can have light and maybe cook up some coffee."

Renata alighted and straightened her skirt. She held out a hand to Bonnie and helped her out of the wagon.

The two women looked at the broken wheel and then at Slocum.

"My, you're tall," Bonnie said.

"Yes'm," answered Slocum.

Renata giggled and grasped Bonnie's hand. She led her away in their hunt for stones to make a fire ring. Slocum heard their titters and whispers as he watched Obie open the long toolbox on the side of the wagon. He propped up the lid with a stick that was inside and rummaged around until he pulled out a hammer, pliers, and three spokes that had been shaped and smoothed by a lathe.

Slocum hobbled all the horses and lay his bedroll on the bare ground next to a large boulder that offered some protection. Then he walked over to Obie, who was repairing the broken wheel.

"I wouldn't light a fire tonight, Obie," he told the wagon driver.

"No? Can't make no coffee without fire."

"You'll draw Apaches like moths to that fire, Obie."

Obie looked up from the rim and spokes.

"By Jiminy, I think you're right. Never thought about 'Paches. Thought we'd left them in the dust."

"They have horses, and they can see fire miles in the dark. A fire would be like a red light on a whorehouse."

Obie cackled a scratchy laugh.

"You're right, o' course. No fire. Just hardtack and maybe a swaller of water."

"I'm going to turn in," Slocum said. "It's been a long day."

"Gals will sleep in the wagon. I'll take old Tom out and lay him out nearby, and I'll sleep underneath the wagon."

Slocum walked off and lay atop his blankets after stripping off his gun belt. His rifle lay next to him and he used his saddlebags for a pillow. He saw the two women peek out of the wagon after Obie removed the dead body. He could not see the expressions on their faces, but he heard them tittering long after he closed his eyes.

Slocum fell asleep to the soft whispers of the women and their muffled giggles from inside the covered wagon.

He dreamed of broken guns and cartridges molded out of clay. He dreamed, too, of hawkeyed men at saloon tables all looking at him as he tried to run. His feet were mired in quicksand, and then he was transported to a grassy glade where he lay in tall red grass next to a stream that made no sound. Next, he saw worms the size of Mexican gourds crawl over his chest and down to his crotch. They wiggled and touched his shirt with flexing fingers.

Around midnight, in the midst of Slocum's dreams, he awakened to hot breath on his face and hands clutching at his clothing. One hand roamed down to his crotch, and when he opened his eyes, he saw one of the women lying beside him, clad in only a thin chemise.

"Bonnie?" he whispered.

"Yes," she hissed. "I want you, Mr. Slocum. I couldn't help myself."

She squeezed his genitals and he felt his prick harden and unfold like a knife blade. She rubbed him and grasped his stalk until it was pressing against the crotch of his trousers.

She leaned over and kissed Slocum on the lips, pressing against him as she continued to grope him.

"Oh, I want you so much," she whispered into his ear.

Slocum cocked his head to pick up the sound of Obie's snoring coming from beneath the wagon. At least, he thought, someone was asleep.

"It's going to be difficult unless I can shuck these duds," he said.

Bonnie giggled, but the sound didn't carry far. She sat up, then bent down to unbutton Slocum's trousers. She felt down his leg with one hand until she touched one of his stovepipe boots.

"You sleep with your boots on," she said.

"Out in the open, I sure do," he said. "Move aside and I'll tug 'em off."

She plopped over and pulled her chemise over her head. Slocum, like a man rowing a boat, leaned down and

loosened his boots, then shucked them off. Bonnie un-
buttoned his shirt as he stared at her naked body in the
moonlight.

Her pert breasts jutted from her chest as he slipped out
of his shirt. She was frantic as she sidled onto his blanket
and settled her buttocks between his legs.

His cock swelled and stood straight up. She raised her
bottom, then slid onto it, her bent legs spread wide. He felt
his prick slide through the folds of her pussy and plunge
into the wet warmth of her cunt.

Bonnie let out a long sigh as she impaled herself on his
member, then wriggled her bottom around in a little circle.

"Oh my," she cooed, "that feels so good, John. Heaven."

She raised and lowered herself so that his cock stroked
her clitoris. She spasmed as an orgasmic convulsion shuddered through her loins.

Surprised that she had come so fast, Slocum reached
out and grasped her hips. He drew her down to him and
kissed her as he thrust his own hips upward, driving deep
into her vulva.

Bonnie shuddered again and grasped his shoulders with
both hands, her fingernails digging into his flesh.

"Yes, yes," she breathed and pumped up and down on
his oil-slick cock.

"Easy, or I'll spill all I've got real quick," he warned.

She slowed down and rose and fell on his stalk while
rocking back and forth gently atop his loins.

Bonnie released her grip on his shoulders and just let
her hands brace her as they flattened atop his blanket.

He looked up and saw that her eyes were closed. He felt
the pleasure of his embedded cock as it continued to swell
and throb like some growing snake inside the moist hot
cavern of her pussy.

She pumped up and down and squirmed as she sought
to have his engorged cock touch every fiber of her pussy.

They both stopped for a moment as they heard a rustle of cloth and the scrape of a body on wood.

Bonnie looked up, toward the wagon, and saw a white shape emerge from the back of the wagon.

"Uh-oh," she said.

"What?" Slocum asked.

"Renata," Bonnie said. "She's awake and I think she's coming this way."

Slocum listened. He heard the pad of bare feet striking the ground.

He smiled.

"The more the merrier," he said.

Bonnie stiffened and slapped him lightly on the chin.

Then she began to pump up and down with quick moves.

The sound of padding feet grew louder as Renata ran over the ground. She hiked up her flannel nightgown and dashed toward Bonnie and Slocum as if on a mission of mercy.

Bonnie's eyes flared with starlight. They were wide open and her cheeks glistened with fresh sweat as she shivered with another orgasm.

Slocum steeled himself to hold his seed.

He knew there was more woman to be had, and he didn't want to spend himself just then and miss the opportunity to pleasure Renata.

3

Renata rushed up to the two lovers and stared down at them. She huffed because she was slightly short of breath.

"Well," she said, "you two seem to be enjoying yourselves."

"Immensely," Bonnie said.

"You little traitor," Renata hissed, "sneaking off like that and not waking me up."

"Want to join us?" Slocum said, a smile flickering on his lips.

"How?" Renata asked as she squatted down next to Slocum's bedroll.

"You can take turns," he said.

"When I'm finished," Bonnie said as she dropped once again on Slocum's cock.

"When will that be?" Renata asked.

Bonnie didn't answer, but gasped as still another orgasm rippled through her loins.

Renata pulled her gown up over her head and tossed it

15

on the ground. She stood naked, and Slocum saw the graceful curves of her body, the taut breasts, the jutting nipples, the dark thatch between her legs. Desire flooded him even as Bonnie fell against him, gasping with the pleasure of her climax.

"Well?" Renata said. "Don't I get a turn with Mr. Slocum?"

Bonnie rose and looked at her naked friend.

"Oh, I suppose so," she said. "You're wicked, Renata."

"Get off him," Renata said and moved a step forward.

Bonnie raised her buttocks and unimpaled herself from Slocum's cock. She rolled off his belly and stood up on shaky legs.

"Make it quick, Renata. I'll want more. It's been a long time."

"For both of us," Renata said as she squatted, then threw a leg over Slocum's loins and straddled him. Her hand felt around for his stalk and grabbed it as she lowered her thatched cunt to its throbbing swollen tip.

"I've never watched before," Bonnie said. "Do you mind, John?"

"Not if it gives you pleasure," he said.

"We'll see," Bonnie said.

Renata raised and lowered herself, plunging Slocum's cock in and out of her steamy cunt. His flesh smacked against hers and Renata's back arched as she felt the swollen member deep inside her pussy.

"Oh, this is wonderful," she said, more to herself than Slocum or Bonnie.

"Have you come yet?" Bonnie asked.

"Not yet. But I feel it. I really feel it."

Slocum thrust upward with his hips and drove deep inside Renata. She shuddered as an electric spasm ripped through her cunt and rippled up her spine. She let out a soft scream and fell against Slocum, her breasts mashing against his chest.

She wriggled so that her nipples hardened. Slocum clasped each cheek of her buttocks and pumped up and down, holding her tight, diving deeper into her warm wet cunt.

Renata climaxed again and then rolled off the blanket, Slocum's cock still buried in her pussy.

"I want you on top of me," she whispered.

The ground mashed into her back and she felt the sting of grit and small pebbles.

Slocum disengaged himself and pulled her onto the blanket.

"No use lying on the ground," he said.

Renata laughed.

"Thanks," she said.

She spread her legs wide, and Slocum looked down at her sloping flat tummy and the dark thatch between her legs. He straddled her and lowered himself until the head of his prick touched the soft folds of her cunt. She reached for him and pulled the head inside her. Slocum pushed and lowered his hips at the same time. He slid into her steamy cunt with ease, and her legs rose slightly as he plumbed the depths clear to the tip of her womb.

Bonnie watched the two in rapt fascination. Her eyes glittered in the moonlight.

An electric orgasm rippled through Renata's body, and she let out a soft scream of pleasure. Slocum increased the speed of his plunge and she climaxed again as Bonnie writhed with desire.

And Obie snored on, deep asleep.

Slocum bent down and kissed Renata's breasts, laving his tongue over her taut nipples. Her lithe body undulated as he continued to pump into her with slow, sure strokes.

They kissed and she sighed when he raised his head to look at her.

Her body bucked with another jolting orgasm and she clung to his buttocks, holding him tight against her loins.

Bonnie's heart fluttered, and she stroked a finger along Slocum's leg as if to draw energy from touching him.

"He's good, isn't he, Renata?" Bonnie said.

"He's more than good. He's marvelous."

"I agree," Bonnie said.

"Let me have it, John," Renata said. "I want your milk to explode inside me."

"You might get a baby," he said.

"I don't care."

"You're the boss," he said, but he knew she wasn't. Some women went half-crazy when they were coupled with a man. They lost all reason, all judgment.

"Do it, John," Bonnie said, excitement in her voice. "Shoot it all into her."

"You stay out of this," Renata said.

Slocum increased the speed of his strokes. He felt her pussy rise up and squeeze his cock as Renata contracted the muscles in her vulva. Faster and faster he drove into her as she tightened down on him and wrapped her legs around his waist.

Her hands roamed up to his back and she held on as if she were bulldogging a steer.

"Oh, oh, oh," she exclaimed as her body convulsed in the spasms of climax.

Slocum felt the seeds rush from his sac and spew through his cock. There was that blinding moment of pure ecstasy as he shot sperm into her cunt, splashing her womb with millions of tiny swimmers. He floated above her for a long moment, and she clung to him as her body quivered against him. He fell atop her, covering her body with his and mashing her breasts.

Bonnie looked at their faces and knew that they had gone mindless in the throes of their shared ecstasy.

She let out a breath and gulped in air to replace it.

"I bet that was nice, Renata," Bonnie said, and it sounded snide to Renata.

But she was on another plane and didn't mind. She felt the warmth of Slocum's seed and that was enough to numb her senses into a state of lassitude.

"Finished, John?" Bonnie asked.

"Yes, for a time. You and Renata better get some sleep and I'm plumb tuckered out."

"I want more," Bonnie said.

Slocum slid off Renata and stood up. He pointed to his crotch.

"He's plumb tuckered out, too, Bonnie. Get some sleep."

Bonnie rose up and stood.

"Well, I never . . ." she said.

"Oh, Bonnie," Renata said. "You're never satisfied. That's why you can't keep a man."

"You little bitch," Bonnie said. "How can you say such a thing to me? I'm your friend."

"And that's what a friend does, you witch."

Renata got to her feet. She doubled up her fists.

Slocum stepped between them.

"No fighting," he said. "You gals get some sleep. You're both worn out."

"I could last all night with you, John," Bonnie said, softening.

"That's enough for one night, Bonnie," Slocum said. "Now get back in that wagon before I spank you."

Bonnie's eyes brightened.

"Oooh," she exclaimed.

Renata spat out of the side of her mouth in disgust.

She gathered up her gown and slipped it back on.

Bonnie stood there for another few seconds, then

stooped over and picked up her nightclothes and slipped them back on.

"Maybe in town . . ." she said to Slocum.

"Maybe," he said. He began to put on his black pants and shirt. He pulled on his boots as Bonnie walked back to the wagon.

Slocum sat down and waited until it was quiet again. Then he plucked a cheroot from his pocket, lit it with a lucifer, and smoked.

Halfway through his cigar, he heard a muffled sound. Instinctively, he reached for his gun belt and unwrapped it.

He peered into the darkness in the direction of the soft sound.

His hand slid to the handle of his bowie knife. He saw a silver flash in the moonlight.

Then one of the shadows grew larger and started toward him.

Slocum drew his knife, and stubbed out his cheroot.

The shadow crept closer and he saw the form of a man, who held a blade in his hand.

Slocum lay flat and the shadow began to run toward him.

Ten feet away, he saw the Apache, silent as a cat, running toward him at full speed, running toward the hobbled horses.

When the Apache was two yards away, Slocum rose up and held the big blade at his waist, ready to strike.

4

The Apache's arm rose up and Slocum saw the knife in his hand poised to strike. Slocum went into a crouch and stepped into the charge, arms widespread like a pair of giant pincers.

Slocum bowed his head and drove into the Apache's midriff. At the same time, he reached up and grabbed the man's wrist above the hand that held the blade. The Apache twisted away as Slocum swung his knife in a tight arc.

The two men grappled and turned in a half circle.

Slocum felt the hot breath of the Apache brave on his face as both struggled to gain an advantage over the other.

Neither man said a word. The only sound was their heavy breathing as they tugged and pushed at each other in a fight to the death.

The Apache grabbed Slocum's wrist to keep from getting stabbed. His grip was strong, but Slocum jerked his knife hand away and staggered out of reach for a second or two. The Apache swung his knife in a wide arc. The blade swished past Slocum's face and he reached out, grabbed the Apache's arm, just above the wrist. He squeezed and twisted, but the knife didn't fall from the brave's hand. Instead, the Apache jerked free and circled Slocum, his knife poised like a snake to strike.

Obie stopped snoring.

His eyes opened. He saw only the blackness of the bottom of the wagon bed and a few stars in a small portion of the sky. But instinctively, he knew something was wrong. He heard the muffled sounds of a scuffle and touched the stock of his rifle lying alongside his bedroll. The sounds did not make sense at first, but he came fully alert and crawled out from under the wagon, the rifle in his grip.

The Apache, wearing only a loincloth, moccasins, and a headband, lunged at Slocum full force, his knife poised just above his shoulders, his hand drawn back like a prizefighter's fist as he snarled under his breath. Slocum stared death in the face just then, and for a split second he thought he would be opened up like a butcher's carcass.

At the last moment, Slocum ducked and dodged. It was purely instinctive, he knew, but it saved his life. The Apache hurtled past as Slocum whirled and slashed at the Apache's midsection. The Apache's forward momentum caught him by surprise and he lost his footing for a moment.

Slocum sliced a thin cut in the Indian's side, and knew that it was not enough.

The Apache whirled to counter Slocum's attack. That was his big mistake.

Slocum brought the big blade up and swiped it across the warrior's forehead, just above the eyebrows. He hit hard and the blade of the bowie slashed a deep cut in the Apache's skull. Clear to the skull bone. Blood gushed from the long wound and dripped into the warrior's eyes. The Apache was blinded and staggered under the force of the blow. He tried to wipe the blood from his eyes, but they had filled up and rendered him totally blind.

The warrior regained his balance enough to turn and brace himself against Slocum's rush. But he was not fast enough. Slocum brought his blade up from knee-high and drove it into the Apache's gut. The blade sank in to the hilt. Blood squirted from the brave's belly button and he doubled up both from pain and the shock of the wound. Slocum twisted the knife blade and sawed sideways, first to the right, then to the left. The bowie knife cut both ways and entrails began to squeeze through the wound like the slimy coils of a skinned snake.

The brave doubled up and dropped to his knees, his intestines exploding through the gaping wound. Slocum withdrew his knife and stepped in close. He pushed the brave's head back with his left hand and slashed at the exposed throat with the bowie. A gaping wound opened up and a waterfall of blood gushed out as the Apache's eyes rolled back in their sockets and he could no longer draw or expel his breath. He made a gurgling sound and fell forward, lifeless.

Thirty yards away, three shadows rose up against the black skyline. Slocum heard the pad of moccasined feet. He sheathed his knife and drew his Colt .45. Then, a shape appeared beside him and he caught sight of Obie out of the corner of his eye.

Obie raised his rifle to his shoulder.

"I got him in my sights," Obie said, and Slocum heard the snick of metal as Obie cocked the hammer back on his rifle.

Slocum cocked his pistol and raised his arm. He drew a bead on the warrior to the left of the other two and held his breath as he lined up the rear buckhorn with the front blade at the muzzle.

Obie fired, and Slocum saw one of the braves clutch his chest and pitch forward.

"Got him," Obie said, and levered another cartridge into the firing chamber of his rifle.

Slocum squeezed the trigger and saw the blast of orange and blue flame as burning powder propelled the .45-caliber lead projectile from the barrel. The bullet smacked into the warrior's chest, splitting the breastbone and flattening against his backbone. The man dropped like a sashweight to the ground, and as Obie took aim on the third man, Slocum thumbed the hammer back. The cylinder spun and seated with another bullet in firing position.

Both men fired at the same time. Both bullets caught the last brave in the chest. His body twisted with the impact of two bullets and blood gushed from a pair of holes. He slowed, but his forward momentum carried him another two or three feet and then he crumpled, dead before his body struck the ground.

There was a long moment of silence as wisps of white smoke drifted upward in the still air. They hung like tattered cobwebs, white against the blackness of night.

Obie was the first to break the silence.

"Whew," he exclaimed in a breathy whisper, "looks like we got 'em all. How many? Four?"

"Four," Slocum said.

The two men walked toward the brave that Slocum had killed with his knife.

Obie turned him over, saw the blood turning to jelly on the Apache's face.

He bent down to examine the wound above the Indian's eyebrows.

"Where'd you learn to do somethin' like that?" he asked.

"In a knife fight, you cut where you can," Slocum said. "He wasn't looking for it."

"I never saw nothin' like it. You blinded the bastard and then gutted him like a fish."

Slocum walked away, and looked at the other three braves they had shot.

All were dead.

Obie followed him and examined the bodies.

Then, he looked closely at one of them and turned him over with the toe of his boot.

"Well, I'll be damned," Obie said.

Slocum came up beside him and looked at the dead man.

"That's no Apache," Slocum whispered. "He's dressed like one, but . . ."

"No, it ain't," Obie said. He bent down to look at the dead man's face. "That's a Mex, name of Fidel Sanchez. Half-breed I reckon."

"He looks like a white man with a tan," Slocum said.

"Mother's Irish, his pa was a Mex."

"You know him."

"He worked for Orson Canby, far as I knew."

"That's the man who contracted for the horses I'm bringing to Deadfall," Slocum said.

"Well, then, you got trouble," Obie said.

"How so?" Slocum asked as the two men stood up straight.

"Canby owns a big part of the town. He's a snake. I wouldn't trust him far as I could throw that wagon yonder."

"Looks to me like he might be a double-crosser," Slocum said.

"You got that right. Double-cross is Canby's middle name. You watch him real close. And if I was you, I'd watch my back, too."

"A drygulcher?" Slocum said.

"You'll be lucky if you ride out of Deadfall with the money he pays you. There's a lot of graves in that town where backshot men lie. All of 'em had dealings with Canby."

Slocum's jaw hardened.

He let out a breath through pursed lips that sounded like a raspy whistle.

What had he gotten himself into with this horse deal?

Obie looked at him and shook his head.

"Yes sir, John, you're dealin' with a man who's tight-fisted as a parson and hires gunslingers to do his dirty work."

"Thanks for warning me," Slocum said as he holstered his pistol.

"Was I you, I'd turn right around with them horses and go back where you come from," Obie said.

"No, I'll see it through. There's money owed and I'm a man of my word."

"Well, Canby sure ain't," Obie said.

The two men walked back toward the wagon, where the two women were huddled together, peering out at them like a pair of frightened owls.

Obie walked over to them and began explaining that they were packing up and leaving. Slocum rolled up his bedroll, no longer sleepy, but wound up tight as a coiled spring.

The desert was now a place of death and the horses were spooked. He could still smell the acrid taint of the burned powder and the scent of blood on flesh and sand.

5

The wagon rumbled into Deadfall carrying two dead men and two mail-order brides, both of them still a trifle wet behind the ears.

"What did you want to bring that Mex with us for?" Obie asked as he pulled the team to a halt in front of the Deadfall Hotel.

"I want to see the look on Canby's face when I lay the body out. Where can I find him?"

"Right here in the hotel, or next door at the Wild Horse Saloon, most likely."

Obie set the brake.

Slocum looked beyond the clapboard buildings to the wide valley beyond. The size of the valley was a surprise and so was its green grass carpet, but then he saw the glint of creek waters on two sides, an oasis in the desert, he thought.

The creeks meandered through the valley and were widely separated. He could see men squatting beside both of them with dark gold pans. They dipped their pans into the gravel and water, then agitated the pans with both hands. The pans tilted to let out the water in gradual sloshes, while the gravel and dirt remained in the pan.

"That's a hard way to make a living," Slocum said as he and Obie climbed down off the wagon and walked to the rear. "Where do those creeks come from?"

"Underground springs, I hear tell," Obie said.

"I've never seen anything like it. Not in any desert."

"It is mighty strange," Obie said as he dropped the tailgate and shook the stockinged foot of one of the women.

"The way you came in here, a man riding out there would never see it. I mean, all those tall thin buttes hide the entrance."

"Wake up, girls," Obie said. "We're at your destination. This is Deadfall."

He turned to Slocum.

"Man who found it wasn't lookin' for gold," he said. "He was huntin' and follered the tracks of some strange beasts. Army had cut 'em loose and they was wanderin' out here like big old ghosts."

"What were they?" Slocum asked.

"Camels."

"Camels?"

The women stirred inside the wagon. Slocum could see their white gowns, bare arms, fluttering hands.

"Yep, camels. Mean, ornery animals, just a-brayin' like Missouri mules. The man roped one and it bit a chunk out of his arm and kicked him square in the balls. But there were other critters here, too, and he cut deadfalls and trapped bear and antelope, I reckon, and found gold in one of them creeks one day."

"What happened to the man?"

"Oh, he stayed on while the town was buildin' up. Had him a claim and all. Then, one day, he warn't here no more.

That happened right after Canby come here and started gobblin' up claims and settin' up ways to steal money from the prospectors. Old Clem Newcomb had maybe the richest claim and then he warn't here no more."

"You think Canby killed him?"

"I ain't sayin'. Nobody is, but there's a unmarked grave somewhere out in the desert, and folks think Clem is six feet under."

Two men emerged from the hotel as the women, dressed now and pulling their carpetbags from the wagon, fluffed their hair and looked around. The men were wearing clean simple clothes, checkered shirts and denims, work boots. They were young and thin, with pale faces, no tan on their hands. They looked like indoor men to Slocum, barflies or card dealers.

Slocum and Obie pulled the body of the Mexican from the wagon. The dead man was stiff as an iron rail. Slocum tugged on one boot, Obie the other. When the corpse was halfway out, Obie walked to the tailgate, and as Slocum pulled on both legs, Obie grabbed the slain shotgun rider by the shoulders and then they laid him out flat on his back in the dirt of the road. Finally, they pulled the body of Sanchez out of the wagon in the same manner and laid his corpse beside Tom Nixon's.

"Damn, Obie," one of the two men remarked, "you deliverin' dead bodies now?"

Obie looked up at Earl Cassaway and squinted.

"Earl, ain't you got no respect for the dead?" Obie said.

"Hey, ain't that Sanchez there?" the other man said.

"That's Sanchez under that 'Pache paint all right," Obie said. "And my shotgunner, Tom Nixon, if it's any of your business, Roddie."

Roddie Nehring pinched his nose as the stench of the two dead men reached his nostrils.

"I bet you got a good story to go with them corpses," Earl said.

"Go get Canby," Obie said. "I'll tell it to him."

"That's Mr. Canby to you, Obie," Earl said, "and he ain't up yet most likely."

"Then you boys can just sniff these dead men till he comes down," Obie said.

The two men shifted their glances to the horses.

"Them your horses, mister?" Roddie said to Slocum.

"For the time being," Slocum said.

"You aimin' to sell 'em?" Earl said.

"They're already sold," Slocum said. His tone was amiable, but the two men scowled under the withering glance of the tall man in black. They both eyed his pistol with bland vacant eyes, and Slocum knew he was being checked out by two gunfighters with less experience than he.

Morning shadows inched along the street of clapboard and adobe buildings. Men began to gather in front of the hotel. Several looked down at the two dead bodies and shrank away as if tasting poisonous air.

Bonnie and Renata stood there with blanched faces and puzzled expressions in their eyes. They searched the faces of the men as if hoping for recognition until one man drifted down the street and wended his way through the gathering assemblage of gawkers.

"Miss Bonnie," he said, "I'm Billy Joe Foster."

"Why, hello there, Billy Joe," Bonnie cooed, liquid honey dripping from her words. "I'm mighty pleased to meet you."

Renata stepped up to Billy Joe impatiently.

"Where's my man, Mr. Devlin?" she asked, her face darkened by the hand she brought to her forehead to shade her eyes from the sun. "Harlan Devlin."

The two gunfighters chuckled and looked at each other for a brief moment.

"Devlin?" one of them said. "Why, he's hangin' around over yonder."

The other man pointed to a gallows tree down the street. A man's body hung from a rope and was slowly turning in the slight breeze that blew through the valley.

"He stole a horse and got caught last night," the first man said. "He was tried and convicted and hanged real early this mornin'."

Renata gasped, then burst into tears.

Bonnie put an arm around Renata's shoulder and drew her close, patted her on the back of the head.

"There, there," she said. "It's not the end of the world."

"Yes it is," sobbed Renata.

Bonnie looked over at Billy Joe. "I'm lookin' for my man, too," she said. "Mr. Hornaday. Any idea where he might be?"

"Yep," one of the men said. "He's in the hoosegow. He'll hang in the mornin'. He helped Devlin steal that horse."

Bonnie's face went pasty with shock. She didn't cry. She just blinked her eyes and appeared to shrink inside her frock.

"What'll we do?" she asked. "We have no money, no place to stay."

The question was asked of no one, but the men in front of the hotel looked at Obie and he looked off in the distance.

Finally, Obie spoke up.

"There's other women here," he said. "Single gals. Orson Canby can put you up and give you jobs. You'll eat and have a roof over your heads."

"Who's Orson Canby?" Renata asked.

"Why, he practically owns the whole town. This is his hotel and he has a saloon and boardinghouse, a gambling hall, among other establishments."

"He's the man who's buying these horses from me," Slocum said.

As if on cue, the hotel door opened and a man stepped out. The two men stepped aside.

"What's going on here?" the man asked. Then he saw Slocum and the four horses.

"You Slocum?" he said.

"I am."

"I'm Orson Canby. If those horses are up to snuff, I'll pay you what I owe."

Then Canby's gaze shifted to the two men laid out on the ground.

"What's going on?" he asked.

"Tom Nixon was kilt by Apaches," Obie replied. "And the other man was with 'em." Obie fixed Canby with a steady gaze. "I believe the Mexican worked for you, Mr. Canby."

"I never saw that man in my life," Canby said.

Slocum knew that Canby was lying. He felt a tick of warning deep inside his brain.

Canby was a large, florid-faced man and wore a suit that was tailor-made, a string tie, and polished boots. He had a large ring on his right index finger, a ruby surrounded by tiny diamonds.

Then Canby saw the two women, and his eyes flashed with light as they widened.

"Are those the gals you brought, Obie?"

"Yes sir," Obie said. "They was set to marry the feller on the gallows and the one you're fixin' to hang."

"Um, too bad," Canby said.

"They ain't got no money and no place to stay," Obie said.

Canby waited a long time before he spoke again. Slocum watched him and felt sorry for the two women. Canby, he figured, was not a kindhearted man. In fact, he was probably ruthless.

All he wanted now was to get paid for the horses and

have a stiff drink of Kentucky bourbon. But he wondered if he could just walk away and leave the two women in the hands of such a man. Whatever he decided, he knew that the longer he stayed in Deadfall, the more dangerous his life would be.

6

Orson walked over to the two women and spoke to them. He looked them over as if they were cattle in an auction barn.

"You gals want to work?" he asked.

Renata and Bonnie nodded.

"Go on down to the boardinghouse and ask for Mrs. Hobbs. Tell her I sent you. She'll get you rooms and assign you to your duties. She cooks a fair meal, so you'll do all right in her care."

Slocum noticed that Canby adopted a different tone of voice with the women. He sounded almost avuncular and kindly.

The women carried their carpetbags down the street to Mrs. Hobbs's boardinghouse.

Canby walked over to the horses, where Slocum was standing with the lead rope in his hands.

"These are trotters," Slocum said. "From Missouri."

"That's what I ordered. They look sound."

Canby opened one horse's mouth and examined his

35

teeth. He felt the chest. He walked around looking at the gelding's legs. He lifted a hind hoof and saw that the horse was recently shod.

"What do I owe you, Slocum?" Canby asked.

"Three hundred."

"I thought two."

"You thought wrong," Slocum said. "It's three. You paid me three and there's three hundred more that's due."

Canby snorted.

He reached into the right front pocket of his trousers and pulled out a money clip made of silver and turquoise. He slipped off the clip and counted out three hundred-dollar bills. He handed them to Slocum.

"Would you mind taking them to my stables a block or so down the street?"

"Not at all," Slocum said.

The two men in front of the hotel watched all this without any expression on their faces.

"I'll show the man where the stables are," one of them said.

"You do that, Hack," Canby said. "Boze, you go with him."

"Yes, sir, Mr. Canby," Walt Bozeman said.

"I think I can find the livery," Slocum said.

"No trouble at all," Rufus Hackberry said. "Just foller us."

Slocum walked down the street leading the four horses and his own, Ferro. Rufus and Walt flanked him, matched his stride step by step. Slocum felt as if he was all but a prisoner of the two men. He saw no reason why they should accompany him to the livery, but apparently it was with Canby's tacit understanding. He was being watched and he didn't like it much.

The two men did not speak nor did Slocum try to engage them in conversation. The silence was so thick he felt he could cut it with a knife and it would fall to the ground like a lump of soft coal.

Walt turned into the stables and Slocum followed him, with Hack right behind him.

There was an old moth-eaten horse tied to a hitchring in front of the stables. It was sway-backed with rheumy eyes, its head drooping, and it stood hipshot as if left there to die.

"Whose horse is that?" Slocum asked Walt.

"It belongs to Mr. Canby," Walt said. "That's the horse what was stolen."

Slocum masked his surprise.

"Why would a man steal such a sorry horse?" Slocum asked Hack.

"You ask too many questions, mister," Hack said.

"Well, that horse isn't worth stealing," Slocum said as they entered the darkened stable.

"Feller," Hack said, "just put up those horses and don't worry none about that stolen horse."

Shafts of sunlight beamed through the walls and the roof of the stable. Dust motes spun and danced in the glowing light like ghostly fireflies. Slocum led the horses to stall doors that were open and put each one inside. There was water and grain in each stall. Ferro pawed the dirt floor as he waited for Slocum to lead him to a feed trough.

Hack and Walt closed the stall doors. Slocum found another empty stall, where he led Ferro. He unsaddled the horse and slipped off his bridle after hefting his saddlebags over his shoulder and slipping his Winchester from its sheath. Ferro began to nibble at the grain as Slocum walked back out and closed the stall door.

He saw movement at the far end of the stable and looked toward the doors.

A tall slender woman was standing there with a sleek gelding that had four white stockings and a star blaze on its forehead. She held a curry comb in her hand and held the horse steady with a halter rope. Sunlight spun radiance through her dark hair, and when she turned to look at Slocum, he saw her breasts taut against her checkered blouse.

He stood there, transfixed by the beauty and grace of both the horse and the woman.

"You finished here, pilgrim?" Hack said to Slocum.

Slocum fixed both men with a hard stare.

"You boys run along," Slocum said. "I'll be around for a time."

"You got your money," Walt said. "No need to stay in town long."

"I'll be the judge of that," Slocum said, and the two men twitched under the glare of his withering glance.

But they turned around and walked out of the stables. At the front doors they turned and looked back, but Slocum was already walking toward the woman at the far end of the livery.

"I was wondering if you were one of Canby's boys," she said, a slightly mocking tone in her voice.

"My escort," he said.

"I saw the horses you brought in," she said. "Canby pay you for them?"

"Yes, he did."

"You're lucky. He pays for very little in this town. And when he does pay, it's not usually in coin of the realm."

"What do you mean?" he said. He looked into her eyes. They were brown and shiny like polished kernels of fine dark wood. They flickered with sunlight when she lifted her chin.

"He usually pays off in lead," she said. "He's a snake."

"What are you doing here?" he asked.

She looked at the man in the black clothing, her gaze frank and noncommittal, as if she were studying the lines and carriage of a fine horse.

"My brother has a mine here. I help him sometimes. But mostly, I mind my own business and ride my horse outside of this valley. I love this country. It's wild and untamed and you can feel the tug of ancient hands at your shirttails when the wind is up."

"It is beautiful country, but there are Apaches out there, even if you don't see them."

"The Apaches just want to be left alone," she said. "They want nothing from me. I see them every so often and I wave to them."

"Do they wave back?"

She laughed, and her laughter was pleasant and musical.

"Yes, they do, sometimes," she said.

She began to stroke the horse's rump with the curry comb.

"I'm John Slocum," he said.

"My name's Laura. My friends call me Laurie. Laurie Taylor. My brother's name is Harvey. I call him Harve for short."

"Pleased to meet you, Laurie," Slocum said.

"Are you a gunfighter?" she asked. "You look like one."

"It's sometimes wrong to put a brand on a man because of how he looks."

"True. But you still look like a gunfighter. It's also obvious you know good horseflesh when you see it."

"I trade horses," he said.

"No gunfights?"

"Only when necessary," he said.

She stopped combing her horse and looked at him again. This time her eyes searched the chiseled features of his face and her lips curled in a smile that was as fleeting as a spring rain on dry prairie.

"I just came back from an early morning ride," she said. "That's a fine horse you have there in the stall. Would you be staying in town long enough to ride with me tomorrow morning?"

He was surprised at her boldness.

"I would make a special point of it," he said.

"Meanwhile, maybe you'd like to walk me home. I have coffee and whiskey. My brother's working his claim and I could use some company."

"It would be my pleasure," he said. "I was going to the saloon to rinse the dust out of my throat with some Kentucky bourbon."

"Harvey keeps Old Taylor in the cupboard. Would that suit you?"

"Coffee would be fine," he said. "The sun hasn't even reached the rimrock yet."

"Fine. I'll put Lancer in his stall and we'll go to my house."

"You're very kind," he said as she turned her horse in to the stall and hung the curry comb on a nail.

"Let's say I'm interested in you, John Slocum. I want to know more about you."

"I'm at your disposal," he said, and bowed slightly as she latched the door to her horse's stall.

A stable boy appeared from the back lot, a pitchfork in his hands.

"Mornin', Miss Taylor," he said. "I didn't know you was back."

"Johnny," she said, "this is John Slocum. That tall black horse is his. Make sure he has plenty of grain and you might rub him down."

"Yes'm, I sure will. Howdy, Mr. Slocum. I'm Johnny Crowell. I take care of the stables here."

Slocum followed Laurie out of the livery and onto the street. She turned to wait for him and then she took his arm and patted the back of his hand.

"This should set the town folk to talking," she said as they passed by log buildings.

People in the stores were staring at them. Laurie flashed her enigmatic smile at them and Slocum smelled the scent of her perfume as they passed the gawkers.

The town was still half asleep, but the shadows on the bluffs and the canyon walls were slowly inching down the red and yellow rocks. The air was fresh and clean, and there was a lightness to Slocum's step that he had not felt in many days.

7

Laurie's log cabin was set apart from the other dwellings erected under the shadows of the tall buttes. It was a simple, homespun structure that appeared solid and livable with a small porch and overhanging roof. Slocum could not see the end of the long valley, but he saw men working the streams and moving along the stone face of the buttes with picks and shovels in their hands.

The door was not locked. Laurie entered first and showed Slocum to a large homemade chair with cushions. She sat on a small divan that had been made of pine and was covered with soft material that appeared to have been hand-sewn. There was a sewing machine set against a wall in the front room.

"Coffee or a drink?" she asked.

"Coffee would be fine," he said.

"I left a pot on the stove. It won't take but a minute."

When she returned with a small tray, there were two cups of steaming coffee on it. She handed one cup to

Slocum and sat down with the other. She set the tray on a small coffee table in front of the couch.

Slocum blew on his coffee and sipped from the rim.

Laurie held her cup up to her lips and looked at Slocum through the steam.

"I know who you are, John Slocum," she said, and there was a twinkle of amusement in her eyes.

"I told you my name," he said

"I mean I know who you really are. For years, and ever since we came out here, my brother Harvey has talked about you."

"He has?"

"Yes. You're his hero."

"I'm nobody's hero."

"You were in Abilene down in Texas one time and Harve said you took on a bunch of killers and stood up to them."

"I've been in Abilene," Slocum admitted. "A time or two."

"There was a gang there, and you stood up to them. You helped an old man and his ailing wife drive off those men."

"I remember some of it," Slocum said.

"He saw you face off the worst of those bad men in a saloon and you outdrew and outshot them."

"It's possible," he said.

"And without expecting any reward. You were just performing a kindness, according to Harve."

Slocum said nothing. He sipped his coffee and looked at Laurie over the rim of his cup.

"He said you were quite the ladies' man, too. All the women in town chased after you."

"I think your brother is mistaken," Slocum said. "I don't remember anything like that in Abilene."

Laurie laughed.

"No, John," she said. "Harve remembers every detail

and knew the whole story by the time you came into that saloon, and not only did you stand up to the threats, but outdrew and outshot the bad guys. He has a vivid memory of that day."

Slocum said nothing. There had been so many shoot-outs in his life since the War Between the States. Sometimes they were a blur in his mind, and at other moments, he could recall such encounters in clear detail. He tried not to think of the men he had killed. While it was always in defense of himself or others, he knew the gravity of taking a human life and he did not like that he had to do it. He disliked civilizations for several reasons. In most of the towns, he had encountered jealousy, envy, greed, and avarice, all springing from so-called "civilized" towns and cities.

Laurie drank more coffee and Slocum saw the way her lips parted seductively as she placed them on the rim of the cup. She was a beautiful woman and as graceful as a doe or a swan. He sensed a wildness in her that would never be tamed by any man and that excited him.

"Well, no matter," she said. "But I thought of what Harvey told me when I saw you at the stables and I'm sure you saw that old broken-down horse outside."

"I saw it," he said.

"Can you imagine anyone in their right mind would try and steal such a horse?"

"No, I can't imagine it," he said.

"That was a put-up job arresting those two boys and accusing them of being horse thieves."

"I thought the same thing myself when I saw that horse," Slocum said.

"It's not the first time such a thing has happened," she said.

"What do you mean?" he asked.

"Orson Canby. He's greedy and without scruples. When

he sees a man strike it rich in this valley, he trumps up one charge or another and has the man killed. Executed. Then he takes over the claims and fills his pockets."

"There are such men all over the West," Slocum said, his coffee now cool enough so that he drained his cup.

"Canby runs this town," she said. "Those two men who were with you at the livery work for him. Dirty work."

"I know," he said.

"They spy on the prospectors and report back to Canby. They hanged one man yesterday or early this morning and now they are going to hang another, the dead man's partner. Is there anything you can do to save his life?"

Slocum felt a tightening in his throat and it wasn't from the coffee, which was not that strong.

He looked at Laurie and saw that she was serious about her question.

He let out a breath through his nostrils.

"What do you want me to do?" he asked.

"Don't let Canby hang him. That way he can't jump the man's claim."

"Is there a jail here?" Slocum asked.

"There's a log cabin they use as a jail. There is only one man guarding it most of the time."

"You're asking me to break whatever law there is in this settlement," Slocum said.

Laurie erupted with a harsh laugh.

"Law? There is no law here in Deadfall. Canby is the law and he's as crooked and mean as a snake."

"If I break that man out of jail, Canby and his men will come after me. I'll have to kill them or get killed myself."

"I know it's a lot to ask," she said, "but I deplore what Canby is doing. He wrongfully hanged Harlan Devlin and now he's going to hang Wallace Hornaday. For stealing a horse that's on its last legs."

"There is a fair amount of injustice here, I grant," Slocum said.

"There's a lot of injustice here," she said, and there was a bitter tone to her voice.

"I'll look into it. When are they going to hang Hornaday, do you know?"

"This afternoon, I think. Canby will want as many town folk to witness the hanging and the afternoon is a perfect time. Those two men who were with you will get Hornaday out of jail and lead him to the gallows. Another man, Wilferd Butterbean, will do the actual hanging. He's a fat pig who knows how to fashion a hangman's knot."

"So you've got a guard at the jail and those two jaspers who walked me to the livery. What about Butterbean? Does he pack iron? Wear a pistol on his hip?"

"I don't know if he does or not. He's not much of a man, just a fat little cockroach who picks up Canby's crumbs."

"What about the jail guard? Do you know anything about him?"

"The night guard is a hardcase named Willie Fordyce. He goes off around this time of day and a man named Steve Beck takes his place. Beck is in his fifties, at least, carries a double-barreled shotgun, and sits on a wooden bench all day. He moves the bench around the jail so he can sit in the shade."

"So he's not always out front?" Slocum said.

"No. Sometimes he's on the side of the building, or in the back. It's a small cabin. He could hear if anyone tried to break down the door or if a prisoner was trying to escape."

Slocum looked outside one of the front windows. The sun was rising in the east so he figured the guard would have his bench on the west side of the jail by the time the sun streamed down the valley, which lay in an east-west direction.

"What do I do with Hornaday if I can get him out? And does Beck have a key to the jail?"

"I don't know," Laurie said. "Probably not. There's a big lock on the door. But it looks old. I glance at it every time I pass by."

"So maybe a crowbar could break that lock," Slocum said.

"It looks old and rusty."

"The sun will be up high pretty soon. If I get Hornaday out, what do I do with him? Canby's men will be hunting him. And me, too, most likely."

"He'll probably want to go to his own cabin not far from here," Laurie said. "But that would not be wise."

"You can't put him up here?"

"No. There's just barely room enough for Harve and me. And Harve wouldn't like to attract attention to himself. He thinks he's found a vein in his mine, and once he does, he'll be a Canby target himself."

"This is complicated," Slocum said.

Laurie finished her coffee and leaned back against the divan. She closed her eyes for a moment, then opened them wide.

"There's an old abandoned mine way down at the end of the valley. Some men used to stay there until they were able to haul in timber to build their cabins. Harvey showed it to me. It had a home-made cot and some wooden boxes. Wallace could hide out there. I could bring him food. The mine is deep and he could have a fire at night, cook coffee or boil eggs in the mornings. There are all kinds of utensils there, and a place for the smoke to go and not be seen. Nobody goes there anymore now that we have a hotel and a boardinghouse in town."

"You'd have to take me there once I get Hornaday out. If I get him out."

"Oh, John, could you? Would you?"

He stood up. He towered over the woman on the divan and she looked up at him with the eyes of a child.

"If I get Hornaday out, I'll bring him here and you can show me that old mine."

"Wallace knows about it. He can take you there. It's a long walk and you'd have to be careful. Canby's eyes are everywhere."

"Where is the jail exactly?" he asked.

"Why, it's behind the stables. On the next small street. You can't miss it."

"When people tell me I can't miss a place, it's usually a bad direction."

Laurie laughed.

"You'll find it," she said.

Laurie stood up and stepped close to Slocum. She put her arms around his waist and hugged him.

"I wish you good luck," she said. "And when you get Wallace settled, come back here and I'll have a box of food we can take down there tonight."

He touched the brim of his hat.

"Wish me luck," he said, her perfumed scent still lingering in his nostrils. She was soft and smooth against his body, as supple as a willow branch. She stirred something deep inside him, and he knew right then that he would surely return, whether he was successful in freeing Hornaday or not.

"Don't hold your breath," he said as he walked outside and headed toward town.

She stood in the doorway, and when he looked back, she dangled a sad wave at him. He waved back and stirred the dust with his boots, his mind racing on how to break out a prisoner who was due for a hanging that very afternoon.

He was taking a big chance, he knew, but he had already decided that he would do anything for the beautiful Laurie Taylor.

8

Deadfall was still half asleep as Slocum walked back toward the livery stable. He saw a few people opening storefronts and sweeping the ever-present red dust away from their establishments. He heard the ring of a pick down the valley and saw men leading burros down one of the creeks, while other men flashed their pans in the light of the rising sun and prepared to tackle the back-breaking task of panning for gold in the shining waters.

He turned at the corner where the livery stable was and walked to the next street.

It was small and narrow, but he saw the tiny cabin that served as the town jail.

The old sway-backed horse was still at the hitchrail outside the stables, its head drooped down low to the ground and standing hipshot as if it was sound asleep. Slocum's stomach swirled with pity and anger. As Slocum turned down the back street, he caught a glimpse of Johnny Crowell at the back doors. That reminded him that he must retrieve his rifle, shotgun, and saddlebags before he checked in at the hotel and got a room for the night. He saw no sign of Obie or his wagon until he saw the wagon parked down the back street minus the team and Obie.

He smelled the strong odor of Mexican food cooking at one of the cafés on the back street. Refried beans and chorizos made his stomach churn once again with hunger.

The cabin that served as a jail was set back from the street and he saw the man he took to be Steve Beck moving his crude wooden bench to the west side of the structure. The man had left his shotgun leaning against the wall next to the front door and was dragging the bench around to the side.

Slocum crossed the street at a slow, but steady pace. Out of the corner of his eye, he saw Johnny forking hay from a rick onto a wooden wheelbarrow. Johnny didn't notice him. Behind the corral, the fence was solid, fashioned of two-by-twelve boards. And there were no other nearby buildings with back windows.

He heard the scrape of the bench on the ground as Beck dragged it into the shade.

As Slocum reached the shotgun and leaned over slightly to snatch it up, he heard the bench bang against the sidewall of the jail.

The sun was rising in the east, buttering the narrow street with yellow light.

Beck turned around after setting his bench in position.

He jumped back a half foot when he saw the tall man in the black outfit come around the corner carrying his shotgun.

"What the . . ." Beck uttered.

Slocum smiled at him.

"Have a seat, Mr. Beck," Slocum said.

"What are you doin' with my scattergun, mister?" Beck asked.

"Sit down," Slocum ordered.

He moved close to Beck, the shotgun held slantwise in both hands.

Beck backed up and slowly lowered himself to the bench.

Slocum stood square before him, looking him up and down.

Beck was a small man with a slight paunch that ballooned over his belt buckle. His hair was thinning with streaks of gray and appeared to be plastered down with pomade under his battered felt hat, which was stained with various unknown substances. He sported a scraggly mustache that was as gray as his pale blue eyes, and the eyes were rheumy, as if stung by cigarette smoke. His lips were chapped and cracked, and he appeared to be missing some important teeth when he opened his mouth in a surprised gape.

"Don't say anything, Mr. Beck," Slocum said. "Just listen."

"Mmmff," Beck said as he stared into the green eyes of the tall stranger.

Slocum leaned over so that his face was inches from that of Beck's.

Then he reached down and slipped the guard's pistol from its holster. He stuck the .36-caliber LeMat in his belt.

"Peashooter," he said to Beck.

Beck opened his mouth as if to say something, but Slocum pressed a finger against his lips to warn him not to speak.

"Now, Mr. Beck, do you have a key to that lock on the jail door? Just say 'yes' or 'no.'"

"Y-Yes," Beck said.

"I'll have that key, Mr. Beck."

Beck reached into a pocket of his pants and withdrew a large skeleton key. He handed it to Slocum.

Slocum took the key and stepped away from Beck.

"I have another question for you, Mr. Beck."

Beck seemed to be shivering. His body shook and his eyes glazed over with a film of fresh tears. He nodded in silence.

"Do you know the man who's in this jail? Hornaday? Keep your voice low when you answer."

Beck nodded. "Yes. I know him. He's a prospector. Stole a horse."

"Do you really think Hornaday stole that nag that's tied up in front of the livery? Think hard before you answer, Mr. Beck."

"It don't seem likely. I mean Wallace and Devlin sure didn't need to steal a horse, much less that one."

"So do you know they're going to hang Wallace Hornaday today?"

"Yeah, I know."

"Do you have a conscience, Mr. Beck?"

Slocum's words were crisp and sharp, as if they had been carved out of hickory.

"I reckon," Beck said.

"Do you care that an innocent man was hanged last night and another is due to go to the gallows today?"

"Nothin' I can do about it," Beck said.

"Well, you are going to do something about it, Mr. Beck. Like it or not."

"What's that?" Beck asked.

"You're going to take Wallace's place in that jail cell and wait for the hangman."

"No, I ain't," Beck said.

"Get up," Slocum ordered.

"They'll . . ." Beck started to say, then clamped his mouth shut before he could finish the sentence.

"They won't hang you in Hornaday's stead, Mr. Beck," Slocum said as Beck rose to his feet.

"They'll sure as hell beat me up, thrash me to within an inch of my life."

"I doubt that, Mr. Beck. But I'm locking you in that jail because I didn't want to lay you out with a shotgun butt. I don't want to hurt you."

"You don't know the men who want to hang Wallace. They don't give a damn who they hurt. Me included."

"Just tell them you were outgunned and caught by surprise, Mr. Beck. And"—Slocum paused as he stared into Beck's eyes—"tell them you were overpowered by a man named Slocum."

"You want them to know who you are?"

"I know who they are, Mr. Beck. They might as well know my name."

"They'll kill you for certain sure, Slocum. You don't know these men. Canby especially. They don't have consciences."

"I'm counting on it, Mr. Beck. Let them come after me."

"You want to get killed?"

Slocum laughed a short harsh laugh.

"Not particularly," he said.

He marched Beck to the front of the jail and opened the lock with the key. He swung the door open.

A small man with a wizened face blinked as the light struck him in the eyes.

"Wallace?" Slocum said.

"Yeah. You the hangman?" Hornaday said.

"No," Slocum said. "You come out. Mr. Beck is going in to take your place."

"What?" Hornaday said.

"Move," Slocum said, and shoved Beck through the door. Hornaday stepped aside, then walked toward Slocum.

"Who in hell are you?" Hornaday said as he shielded his eyes from the sun.

"Come with me, Wallace, and just act natural. Keep your mouth shut."

"You goin' to kill me?" Hornaday said.

He was thin and wiry, his face burnished brown by the sun as were his hands and wrists. He wore a faded blue shirt and worn-out duck pants stuffed into work boots. He had traces of blood on his clothing where the rats had bitten him during the night. He looked a wreck, Slocum thought.

"You won't get away with this, Slocum," Beck said, but he shrank back into the cell and cowered there in the dim light.

"If you holler, Mr. Beck, I might just spray you with shot from this scattergun. Just sit down and stay quiet."

Slocum closed the door to the jail and slipped the lock back in place, closed it with a snap.

Beck let out a low moan as the lock clicked shut.

Slocum unloaded the shotgun, cracking it open and ejecting two shells. He also emptied the .36 and took both around to the side of the jail and placed them beneath the bench.

"Come with me, Hornaday," Slocum said, and started to walk around to the stables.

"Where we goin'?" he asked.

"Someplace where you'll be safe," Slocum said.

"Ain't no safe place for me in Deadfall," Hornaday said.

"I know. Just trust me for now," Slocum said.

"Hell, I think you just saved me from getting my neck stretched."

They reached Main Street and Slocum stopped, held Hornaday back with an outstretched arm. Then he stepped out and pointed to the gray horse in front of the livery.

"Did you steal that horse yonder, Wallace?" Slocum asked.

"Hell no. I never stole nothin'. Neither did Harlan, and I see him hangin' from that gallows up the street."

"That's what they were going to do to you," Slocum said.

Hornaday rubbed his neck.

"I know," he said, his voice tight in his throat.

"Just walk with me, Hornaday," Slocum said. "Like we were both going someplace with a purpose."

"Where are we going?" Wallace asked again.

Slocum didn't answer. He felt the heat of the sun on his back and knew that the town was stirring. He did not look back, but walked in long steady strides with Hornaday at his side, as if they were two men going to work somewhere down the long valley.

When they were clear of the town, Slocum headed toward Laurie and Harvey's cabin, where the shadows were still long from the high bluffs that glowed red and pink under the crown of the buttes.

"Why, that's Harve's cabin over yonder," Wallace said as they neared the log hut.

"You do have a friend or two here in Deadfall," Slocum said.

"Mister, I don't know who you are or where in hell you came from, but I'm mighty grateful to be out of that jail."

"If you do what you're told from here on out," Slocum said, "you'll likely live to a ripe old age."

"You a friend of Harve's?" Hornaday asked.

"Never met him," Slocum said.

Hornaday's eyes widened. He was dazed by all that had happened to him and couldn't quite believe that he was a free man.

He couldn't quite believe that he wasn't going to the gallows over a trumped-up crime.

He felt as if he were dreaming, in fact, and the man in the black clothes made all of it seem even more unreal.

He shook his head and pinched himself on the cheek to see if he was actually awake and still alive.

Laurie met them at the door and whisked the two men inside.

Her eyes glowed with an intense light and Slocum felt a warm stirring in his loins. He looked back at the edge of the valley in the direction of where the town ended.

He saw no one.

Laurie closed the door and dropped the latch.

Hornaday appeared to be in a stupor and just blinked his eyes at her, dumbfounded.

She patted Slocum on the arm.

"Any trouble?" she asked.

"Not a bit," Slocum said, and her warm smile was his reward for what he had done.

9

Orson Canby sat at the table in the hotel dining room with Walt Bozeman and Rufus Hackberry, a lit cigar poking from his flabby lips. The waiter had just cleared away their plates and poured fresh coffee into their cups.

Walt, whom they called "Boze," the taller of the two gunmen, rolled a quirly and lit it. Like his cohort, Hack, he was lean and trim, with neat sideburns, a slightly wattled neck with a bandanna tied loosely around it. He wore a Colt .44 on his hip and saw to it that the bullets in his cartridge belt were always shining with a light film of oil.

Hack struck a match and lit Boze's cigarette. He did not smoke, but worried a cut plug of tobacco from cheek to cheek. He slid a spittoon closer to him with the toe of his worn boot. He had a thin mustache and his sideburns flared on the upper edge of his cheek, a rust red, as was the color of his spiky hair.

"What do you boys make of that Slocum feller?" Canby asked as he drew on his chubby cigar.

Boze chuckled under his breath.

"He's a head taller than Hack and me, Orson, but he don't look like much."

"Hack, what do you think of the man who sold me those horses?"

Hack squirmed in his chair and stopped chewing his small cud of tobacco for a moment.

"Like Boze said, he's a tall drink of water and seems to know horseflesh. I didn't like the way he looked at that old flea-bit gelding tied up outside the livery."

"How did he look at it?" Canby asked.

"Like he pitied it," Hackberry said.

Boze nodded in agreement.

"Is he movin' on, you think?" Canby asked.

"Hard to tell," Boze said. "He was talkin' to that Taylor gal when we left. Laurie."

"Hmmm," Canby said. "Maybe he has an eye for the ladies."

"He can eye all he wants," Boze said. "It won't get him much in Deadfall."

Hack laughed and slid his chaw over to the left side of his mouth with the tip of his tongue.

"I sent Whit over to the saloon to fetch Marlene over here," Canby said. "Told her to take a look at them two gals Obie drug in here this morning."

"What you got in mind, Orson?" Boze asked.

"Well, seein' as how they neither one got their man, I thought Marlene might put 'em to work at the saloon, give 'em both cribs so's they can spread their legs for them thirsty prospectors."

"Haw," Hack laughed. "Good idea, Orson. We could all use some fresh meat in town."

Boze laughed, too. "They looked mighty appealing to me," he said.

"Well, Marlene's just the one who can turn them two

gals into greenbacks on their backs," Orson said. He blew a plume of gray-blue smoke into the air above the other two men's heads.

They all looked toward the double-wide doors leading to the lobby of the hotel as Marlene Vanders flounced into the dining room swinging a small clutch bag embroidered with Navajo designs. She looked to be twenty years old, but was pushing thirty. Her dress clung to her slender, curvaceous body as she walked toward the table where Orson and his men sat, as jaunty as if she were even younger than twenty. Her long black hair glistened with the sheen of a crow's velvety wing, and her blue eyes with their long lashes seemed to brighten as she glided toward them on high-heeled patent leather shoes. Her breasts rose and fell with her movements, ample and pert beneath her bright yellow blouse.

"Good morning, fellers," she said, her tone bright as the sun that now streamed through the front windows of the dining salon.

"Get Marlene a chair, Hack," Orson said, and Hackberry rose and grabbed a chair from a nearby table and swung it to an empty spot next to Orson.

"God, it's early," Marlene said as she sat down. None of the men pulled out her chair for her. She reached over to Boze and slipped out his bag of makings and papers. She rolled a cigarette with deft delicate fingers.

When she finished, she dumped the bag of makings on the table and leaned over toward Hackberry.

"You going to light me, Hack?" she said. Her voice was musical with a slight rasp to it. She batted her long eyelashes at the gunman and smiled without parting her lips.

"Sure, Marlene," Hack said. He struck a match as she leaned forward and lit the end of her cigarette.

"Thanks," she said. Then she looked at Orson and the smile vanished.

"You get a girl up early, Orson," she said.

"I get up early and expect the world to follow my example," he said. He drew smoke into his mouth and blew a plume over all their heads.

"Well, I went over to see Carrie at her boardinghouse. Saw the new gals."

"And what did you think?" Orson asked. He raised his coffee cup and sipped from it.

"Both wet behind the ears. But young enough to train. Fair figures. Mad as a couple of wet hens when I talked to them."

"About what?" Orson asked.

"The one named Bonnie saw her mail-order groom hanging from the gallows. The other one, Renata, knows her man is locked up to be hanged this afternoon."

"Perfect," Orson said. "They have no ties here or anywhere else."

"I think they feel stood up," Marlene said and this time her teeth showed when she smiled.

The men at the table chuckled.

"That's a good one, Marlene," Orson said. "They were stood up by a couple of horse thieves."

Marlene seemed to wince at this outright lie. But she knew Orson believed what he was saying and she wasn't going to argue with him.

"The good thing is that they're both flat broke, and when I offered them jobs at the Wild Horse, they seemed interested."

"Did they ask what their chores would be?" Orson asked.

Marlene laughed.

"They did, but I didn't tell them. I just said I needed help serving drinks and sweeping up. Bonnie used to work as a scullery maid in some little town and Renata did laundry for a lumber camp in Missouri or somewhere."

"How far will they go to please these galoots in Deadfall?" Orson asked.

"Once I dress them up and turn them into glitter girls, I think they'll tumble into bed with anyone who wears pants. They'll like the extra money I'll pay them."

"All you got now are a couple of Mex gals that look saddle-sore and tired," Boze said.

"That's right. Maria and Teresa. They have about as much fire as a burned-out match."

Marlene crossed her legs and pulled on her cigarette.

"So you think these two gals can rake in some silver up in their cribs," Orson said.

She looked at her boss and grinned.

"You want to break them in, Orson? They're not virgins, but they're dumb as monkeys. About the world, I mean."

"No, I'll let the boys take on that job," Orson said. "Maybe Cassaway and Nehring would like to wet their whistles and dip their wicks when you got those gals all dressed up."

"Maria and Teresa are going to fit them out this afternoon. They can do any sewing needs to be done."

"You're a good woman, Marlene," Orson said. "Smart in business and tough as nails. Too bad you never found a man."

Orson didn't think he was being condescending, but Marlene's eyes seemed to change color from deep brown to a pale tan as if she had been slapped across the face with a wet hide.

"Let's say I've had a good look at the lives of glitter girls, Orson, and it's not something I'd do myself. I'd rather run a business and I don't like strings. I'm not a puppet."

"No, you're not, Marlene," Orson said. "That's what I like about you. You don't take any shit off of anyone and you run your business the way I like to run mine. So you think those gals will work out at the Wild Horse?"

"I'd bet on it, Orson," Marlene said. "Once they see themselves in the mirror with black mesh stockings, red garters, and short silk skirts with low bodices, they'll fall in love with themselves, and if they don't know how to flirt, I'll teach them."

Hack and Boze laughed.

Orson squinted down at his cigar and took a couple of short puffs. Then he lifted his coffee cup again and drank from it.

"You do know how to flirt, Marline," Orson said.

"And I know how far to go, Orson."

"That you do," Orson admitted.

Marlene smoked and uncrossed her legs. She brushed a strand of hair away from her face.

"Whit said to tell you he's going over to talk to Butterbean."

"What for?" Orson asked.

"He wonders if he has to feed that prisoner you're going to hang this afternoon. What's his name? Hornaday?"

"Wallace Hornaday," Orson said. He slipped a gold watch from his pocket and looked at the time, then stuffed it back, leaving the chain loop dangling.

"Whit said sometimes Butterbean doesn't want to feed a man he's going to hang," Marlene said.

"Yeah, too messy," Boze said.

"You make my stomach turn, Boze," Marlene said.

"Sorry, Marlene," Boze said.

Orson stubbed out the remainder of his cigar and patted his ample belly.

He took another swallow of coffee.

"All right, Marlene. You can go see after those new gals. Good luck."

Marlene mashed her cigarette in the ashtray next to the cigar stub. She stood up.

"I'll get the word out," she said, "that we have some new glitter girls in Gravel Gulch."

"We'll spread the word, too," Hack said.

Orson nodded in approval.

The three men stood up as Marlene rose from her chair. They watched her walk out of the dining room, her hips swaying slightly, her poise unmistakable.

"Boy, I'd like a taste of that," Boze said.

"She'd knee you square in the balls if you laid a hand on her, Boze," Hack said.

Orson said nothing.

He thought of the time when he met Marlene. She was running a saloon in a Texas cow town and was restless. He told her about Deadfall and offered to help set her up in business with a saloon that she could manage and just pay him a percentage of her income. She jumped at the chance. But when he tried to get her into his bed, he was rebuffed and she laid down the law to him in no uncertain terms.

For that, Orson respected her, and since then, their relationship had been strictly business. He liked the money she brought in and she helped make the town habitable. Men needed diversion from the hard work of panning and digging in hard rock, and she provided them with whiskey and women. And the little settlement was growing into a town.

Orson was becoming rich and, he suspected, he would become even richer as men came and went, doing all the hard work and spending their gold in Deadfall.

"I'll see you boys later," Orson said. "Keep your eyes open and let me know what that Slocum feller does while he's here."

"Sure will, boss," Boze said.

"Thanks for the grub," Hack said.

The men parted company in the lobby of the hotel.

Orson walked out and headed for Butterbean's cabin, beyond the boardinghouse.

He wanted to be sure the hanging went off without a hitch.

10

Whit sat on a crude chair in Wilferd Butterbean's small front room. Wil was handling a large stout rope as if it were a snake, twirling it around and wrapping a length of it in tight spirals around the neck of the bitter end.

"Wil, you do that knot real good," Whit said.

"It's an art."

"Gives me the willies," Whit said.

"You got to make the loops strong enough and tight enough to hold as the knot under the criminal's ear snaps the neck. Just like a twig."

Whit shivered with a cold chill up his spine.

Butterbean, a burly, thick-necked man in his mid-forties, pulled the loops tight from end to end. He made sure the loop could be tightened around the neck of the man to be hanged. He wore a gray shirt with no collar and thin duck pants, a pair of lace-up work boots. He sweated profusely.

Whit, in his twenties, was a wan-faced youth with freckles on his face, towheaded, with sprigs of hair that stuck out form his scalp at all angles. He had small tight lips and a button nose that made him look like a boy in his teens.

Butterbean finished the hangman's knot and dropped the rope to the floor. He patted the balding spot in the center of his skull, then fluffed the blond hair that grew long on both sides of his head.

"What you want anyways, Whit?"

"Oh, I darn near forgot, Wil," Whit said. "Do you want me to feed the prisoner any grub before you hang him this afternoon?"

Butterbean thought about it for a second or two.

"No need," he said. "But as long as you're here, you can help me take down that one I hanged yesterday. He's probably startin' to get ripe."

"Jesus," Whit said. "What are you going to do with him?"

"We got to load his corpse in a cart and haul him outside of town."

"Then what?" Whit asked.

"We'll find a butte some distance and pile talus atop him. Ground's too damned hard to dig him a hole."

"I reckon I can help you since I don't have to take any grub over to the jail for Hornaday."

"They's a cart out back, like one of them Japanese rickshaws. You step into the braces and pull it. I'll push if need be."

"You ready now, Wil?" Whit asked.

"Yep. I want to keep that rope I hung around Devlin's neck yesterday. No use a-wastin' it."

"How come you don't use that rope for Hornaday, Wil?"

"I like a fresh rope. I'll wash that other one and retie it when the time comes."

"You like this kind of work, Wil?" Whit stood up and brushed off his trousers, which were clotted with dust.

"I don't mind it," Butterbean said. "It's a thrill when I hear them neck bones crack and know I tied a good knot."

Whit shivered again.

The two walked out of the hut and around back, where there was a small two-wheeled cart with an enclosed square of handles. Whit stepped inside the square and lifted the front bar.

"It is a little old rickshaw," Whit said.

"Easy to pull right now," Butterbean said.

The two walked to the main street of Deadfall and to the gallows. The wood used to build it had seasoned, but there was the smell of death all around it.

Harlan Devlin hung there, his feet drooping about a foot and a half below the trapdoor.

"You just wait here by the corpse," Butterbean said.

Whit pinched his nostrils to shut off the smell of decaying flesh.

Butterbean climbed the stairs and pulled on the rope around Devlin's neck.

He grunted as he pulled the body up through the sprung trapdoor. Then he laid Devlin's body out flat on the deck and began to loosen the knot. He slipped the noose over the dead man's head and then reached up to untie the rope from the overhead rafter. It took him several minutes to loosen the three knots that held the loose end of the rope in place. He coiled up the rope and set it near the steps.

"I'm going to drop him over the side of the platform, Whit. Move that cart out of the way and step aside."

Whit moved the cart and stood well away from the platform.

Butterbean leaned down and felt the back of Devlin's neck. There was a decided crook in it where the spine had broken. Satisfied, he rolled the body over to the edge of the platform, then pushed it off the side.

The corpse landed with a thud, kicking up puffs of dust.

There was the sound of a crack as Devlin's head hit the ground.

"Broke his neck again, by gosh," Butterbean said.

Whit looked at the dead man's face. There was a little blood at the corners of his lips. His face was colorless, bland as week-old bread dough, and his eyes stared into nothingness as flies clotted the moisture, feeding on fluids. Whit turned away and gagged.

Butterbean walked down the steps, holding on to the two-by-four railing for support.

"You grab his feet and I'll lift his shoulders, Whit. Then, we'll dump him into the cart."

Whit did as he was told. He could no longer look at Devlin's face, but held his gaze to his dusty boots.

"You don't put a hood on the men you hang, do you, Wil?"

The two dropped the body into the cart. The cart creaked from the weight of its load.

"I'll pick up my rope on the way back and reset that trapdoor. Maybe oil the mechanism before I drop Hornaday this afternoon."

"Sure," Whit said, and stepped into the square rig of the cart.

"Just head up Main Street and I'll spell you if you get tired," Butterbean said.

Whit pushed on the front bar and the cart started to roll. Butterbean walked beside him. People along the street stared at them and he saw faces in the windows. They passed Mrs. Hobbs's boardinghouse, the Wild Horse Saloon, and the Deadfall Hotel, and cleared the town a few minutes later.

Wil avoided the ruts left by lumber and supply wagons that rolled in from Flagstaff every so often. They walked in drenching sunlight toward several buttes of varying sizes.

Butterbean kept looking back to gauge the distance from the edge of town.

They passed two buttes, rounded one of them, and headed for two smaller ones, Butterbean in the lead.

"They's a good one yonder. I think they's some bones under that talus from previous lynchings," Butterbean said.

Whit puffed as the load became heavier and the strain on his back grew stronger.

"You tired, Whit?" Butterbean asked.

"Plumb," Whit said.

"Set 'er down and I'll pull the cart the rest of the way," Butterbean said.

Whit halted and dropped the bar. He stepped out of the square. Butterbean stepped in and lifted the bar. He walked toward the small butte with piles of rocks along its bottom edge.

"A perfect burial place," he said as they came close to the massive rock face of the butte.

"I'm glad we don't have to dig him a grave," Whit said.

They hefted Devlin's body from the cart and carried it to the bottom of the butte. Butterbean kicked away a few stones and then stooped to pick up two loose ones nearby.

"Cover him up with rocks, Whit," Butterbean said. "Completely."

"Yes sir," Whit said.

The two began to pile rocks over the stiff body.

"He sure stinks," Whit said.

"When a man dies," Butterbean said, "there's a muscle in his asshole that loosens up. Devlin took a dump when his neck bone snapped."

"Christ. Yeah, I can smell his shit."

"Something you get used to when you're a hangman," Butterbean said.

"How do you stand it, Wil?" Whit asked.

"I ignore the smells," Butterbean said. He began to

throw more rocks on those already covering the body until it disappeared.

"Keep chunking rocks on this here grave," Butterbean said. "Might keep the coyotes off, might not. But them rocks will turn hot in the sun and make the body decompose faster."

"Horrible," Whit said. "I mean Devlin should be alive, you ask me."

"What do you mean?" Butterbean asked.

"I mean if you think he and Hornaday stole that broken-down old horse, you got to be stone blind," Whit said.

"You better not say that in town," Butterbean said. He was short of breath from the effort of tossing stones on the hanged man's grave.

"Hell, everybody knows that was a put-up job, arresting those two men for stealing a horse."

Butterbean stood up.

"Whit, you want some advice? Keep such thoughts to yourself. If Canby got word that you were saying those men weren't guilty, you'd be dead meat."

"Hell, I can't help what I think," Whit said.

"No, but you can sure as hell keep your mouth shut."

"Somebody ought to do something about this," Whit said. "It—it's an injustice."

Butterbean leaned down and threw another rock on top of the pile. It was now at least two feet high and there was no trace of Devlin's corpse.

"If you're lookin' for justice in Deadfall, sonny, you're in the wrong place. Canby's the law there and you better not buck him if you want to stay alive and keep your skin."

Whit threw another rock on the pile. Butterbean grabbed his arm.

"That's enough," he said. "Enough stones, enough talk. Let's head back to town."

The two walked away from the crude grave.

Then Butterbean looked up at the far buttes all shining in the sun, all flowing into the distance like stone ships on a sand sea.

He shaded his eyes with his hand and pushed the flap of his hat brim back away from his face.

Whit looked up, too.

He saw puffs of white smoke rising from one of the bluffs. When he turned his head, he saw other cloudlets of smoke. Puff, puff, puff.

"What's that about?" Whit asked.

"'Paches," Butterbean said under his breath. "They're talkin' to each other."

"What does it mean?"

"I dunno. I don't read smoke signals, but them Apaches are up to no good. You can bet on that."

"Huh?" Whit said, bewildered. Some of the smoke puffs were close together and some were spaced out from different buttes.

"We'd better skedaddle," Butterbean said. "I got to tell Canby about this."

"What do you make of it, Wil?" Whit asked.

Butterbean picked up the handle of the cart and started walking at a brisk pace toward Deadfall.

"Them Apaches are sure as hell aimin' to do something that ain't good," Butterbean said.

As Whit walked along beside Butterbean, he looked back at the smoke signals. There were several of them and they were far apart, rising from different bluffs.

Then fear struck him. The Apaches were invisible, but he knew they were out there. And they were planning something. He was sure of that. Even in the rising heat of morning, he felt a cold chill steal over his body.

He kept pace with Butterbean.

And they were both in a hurry to get back into the sheltered valley, where they could feel safe.

11

Slocum glanced at the left wall of the cabin.

There, neatly stacked, were his saddlebags, bedroll, with the sawed-off shotgun butt showing in the folded material, and his rifle lying across.

"While you were gone," Laurie said, "I took the liberty of getting your rifle, bedroll, and saddlebags from the stable. I figured you might need them. Especially the bedroll."

"Why?" Slocum asked.

"I don't think you ought to stay in Deadfall until things quiet down," she said.

"Are they noisy?" Slocum asked as Wallace Hornaday stood there, trembling, in the center of the room. He looked lost and bewildered, Slocum thought.

"Oh, there'll be a ruckus once they find out you broke Wallace out of that jail."

"I was going to bunk at the hotel and ride out tomorrow morning." Slocum looked almost as bewildered as Hornaday.

75

"Johnny heard something back at the jail," she said, "and when I walked into the livery, he was all gab about you and Beck being up to something. Then, he said he saw you push Beck into the jail and lead Wallace away after you put that shotgun and Beck's pistol under the bench."

"He saw us?" Hornaday said. "He'll tell Canby for sure."

"Yes, he will," Laurie said. "You'd both better sit down and listen to what I have to say."

She waved Hornaday to the divan, and Slocum sat in the chair he had occupied earlier that morning.

"I'm listening," Slocum said.

"I told Johnny not to say anything right away. He said he had to tell Canby about the jailbreak or Canby would have his hide."

"So he probably ran up the street to tell Canby what I did," Slocum said.

"No, I told him that Canby would find out when the men came to take Wallace to the gallows. I said he didn't need to say anything. As a favor to me. You owe me a dollar, John. I gave a silver one to Johnny to make him hold his tongue."

"Boy, that was right smart of you, Laurie," Hornaday said.

Slocum dug a hand into his trouser pocket and withdrew a silver dollar. He flipped it to Laurie, who sat next to Hornaday on the divan.

She caught it in midair and slid it into the pocket of her blouse. She smiled at Slocum.

"Thank you," she said.

"What now?" Slocum asked.

"I've got flour sacks filled with food for you, Wallace," she said. "John and I are going to take you to a good hiding place at the other end of Gravel Gulch."

"A hideout?" Hornaday said.

"You've got to lay low until all this blows over," Laurie

said. "You'll be safe there, and Harve and I will bring you water and food."

"It's not going to blow over," Slocum said.

Both Hornaday and Laurie stared at Slocum as if he'd just dropped a bomb in their laps.

"What are you saying, John?" Laurie asked when she had regained her composure.

"I mean, as long as Canby is running this town, Wallace here isn't safe. He may not hang you, Wallace, but one of his men might shoot you in the back."

"Boy, you learn fast, don't you, John?" Laurie said.

"Anyone who sets up two innocent men and accuses them of being horse thieves has something bad sticking in his craw. From what I've seen so far, Canby runs the town and he's greedy."

"You got that plumb straight, Slocum," Hornaday said. "Me'n Harlan never came near that horse in town. Next thing we knew, it was tied up at our cabin and Canby's men swarmed all over us like we was dangerous outlaws."

"That tells me that Canby will stop at nothing to get what he wants," Slocum said. He fished out a cheroot from his pocket and bit off the end. He took the tip out of his mouth and set it in an ashtray, then put the cigar in his mouth. He did not light it, but just left it in his teeth, letting the tobacco juices flow over his tongue.

"We'd better get going," Laurie said. "We'll stop by Harve's mine and let him know what's going on. Besides, John, I want you to meet my brother."

"I'm looking forward to it," Slocum said.

Laurie got up and beckoned to the two men to follow her into the kitchen.

There, on a counter, were two flour sacks filled with airtights, bread, biscuits, fried beef, and bacon wrapped in oil paper, and a pair of wooden canteens.

"I'll carry the water," Carrie said. "You can each carry a food sack. That all right?"

"Yes'm," Hornaday said.

Slocum nodded and reached for one of the sacks.

Hornaday grabbed the other sack.

"Wallace, I've got an extra pistol in my bedroom, with a holster and cartridge belt. You might need it."

"I do feel kind of naked, but I've never shot nobody," he said.

"Let's hope you won't have to use it," she said.

They walked back down the hall. Laurie carried the two canteens and slung one on each shoulder. She entered a room while the two men walked on to the front room and set down their sacks near the door.

Laurie came into the room with a holster and gun belt wrapped up in a ball. She handed the rig to Hornaday. He strapped it on and pulled the pistol from its holster.

"This is a mite better'n my old hogleg," he said.

"It's a converted Remington .44," Laurie said. "Shoots straight and has never misfired."

"A lot of gun," Hornaday said as he slipped the pistol back in its holster.

"It's loaded," Laurie said.

Then she looked at the two men and adjusted the canteen straps on her shoulder.

"Shall we go?" she said.

Hornaday and Slocum lifted their sacks from the floor.

Slocum opened the door and held it while Hornaday and Laurie stepped out onto the dirt in front of the cabin. Then he closed the door and slung the food sack over his left shoulder.

"Follow me," she said. "We'll walk next to the big butte on this side and then cross over to where Harve's mine is," she said.

They walked along a worn path next to the other creek.

There were a few men on that side of the canyon valley and they were busy dipping their gold pans into the stream. Apparently, without much luck. One would dip gravel and water, swirl the sediment by tilting his pan one way then another, and peering into the pan as he eliminated small portions of sand and water. Then shook his head when no color showed and repeated the process.

"Howdy, Carl," Laurie said as they passed the man.

"Mornin', Laurie."

He bent down to dip more water and sand into his pan.

They walked about a mile then Laurie turned away from the creek and headed straight for the other buttes that flanked the right side of the canyon. There were miners and prospectors plying the other creek, and some were digging into the base of the butte with picks.

Slocum could smell their sweat as they drew near.

Laurie spoke to none of them, but turned left and stopped in front of a mine adit, a gaping black hole in the side of the bluff, at the very bottom of the butte.

"Drop your sacks," she said. "I'll see if Harvey is inside."

Slocum and Hornaday set their sacks down. They clanked with the airtights.

Laurie disappeared into the cave.

Slocum lit his cheroot and looked around. Men lined the creek while others jabbed holes in the butte with picks. He saw a box of dynamite at one of the camps, stacked with tools and grub and wooden canteens. But so far, he had heard no explosions. Some of the holes were deep; the others were just getting started by men doing backbreaking work.

Moments later, Laurie appeared at the cave entrance, the canteens dangling from her shoulders. Behind her was a man in his thirties, his face covered with grime, his rumpled hat askew on his head. He had black hair and brown eyes. The sleeves of his chambray shirt were rolled up to the elbows, and his hands were infested with dirt and calluses.

"Harve," she said, "you know Wallace, but this is John Slocum."

Harvey's eyes widened.

He stared at Slocum as if he were seeing a ghost.

"Slocum?" he mumbled.

"Pleased to meet you, Harvey. Unless we've met before," Slocum said.

Harvey walked up to Slocum and held out his dirty hand to shake Slocum's.

"No, no, we never met, but I seen you in Abilene. I mean I saw you there. Man, what I saw."

"Now, Harve," Laurie chided. "Don't carry on so."

Slocum shook his hand with a powerful grip.

Harvey grinned wide and pumped Slocum's hand up and down as if he were running for political office.

"I never thought I'd meet you in person, Slocum," Harvey said. "Gawd, it's an honor."

"Harvey . . ." Laurie said.

"I can't help it," Harvey said. "Slocum, I've thought about you for years. Ever since I saw you shoot down those gunmen in Abilene. Man, you sure know how to tame a town."

Slocum pulled smoke into his mouth from the cheroot and took a backward step as if to put some distance between him and the adoring Harvey.

"I've told Harve where we're going," Laurie said. "Wallace, he'll check on you every morning before he comes to his mine here."

"Much obliged," Hornaday said.

"We'll be on our way, Harvey. Don't breathe a word of this to anyone."

"You know me better than that, sis. I know what Canby

tried to do to Wallace and what he did to Harlan. It's a damned shame."

"How's the mine going?" Slocum asked, spewing a plume of smoke into the air.

"I'm gettin' close to a vein, I think. I'm seein' more chunks and flakes."

"You might strike it rich," Slocum said. "I hope so."

"Way I figure it," Harvey said, "there was once a great river running through this valley. It carved out these buttes from pure rock and left lots of gold embedded here and there when it passed through from way up north."

"That's probably what happened," Slocum said. "I've seen other mines in the Rockies that showed the earth was once hot and that gold was liquid, flowing south like water."

"You boys can talk mining and gold some other time," Laurie said. "We've got to get Wallace tucked away safe and set up in his hiding place."

"See you soon, I hope, Slocum," Harvey said.

"Soon," Slocum said. "You can call me John, if you like."

"Yes sir. John."

Harvey grinned. Slocum and Hornaday picked up their flour sacks and followed Laurie as she walked down the butte wall next to the creek.

As they were nearing the end of the valley, Slocum looked up and saw puffs of smoke, bright against the blue sky.

He counted the puffs and made a mental note.

He could read some of the sign and he didn't like what he saw.

Laurie looked up, too.

"Oh, look," she said. "Smoke."

Wallace tilted his head and looked at the puffs of white smoke.

Slocum didn't say anything just then. He just knew those smoke signals meant trouble.

The Apaches were calling out for a powwow in three days.

That much he knew.

Three days, and then what?

He stubbed out his cheroot and tramped on, worry lines furrowing his brow under the brim of his black hat.

12

At the end of the long valley, Laurie turned away from the creek and passed behind the last butte. She walked another two hundred yards toward a smaller butte that could not be seen from the valley.

Beyond the small butte, Slocum saw a low mesa that seemed isolated and out of place among the statuary of elegant buttes. Laurie turned toward the mesa and they passed the butte.

At the foot of the mesa, there was a great pile of rocks, as if part of it had been exploded. They approached the pile of rocks and Slocum saw that they were the remains of a small butte that had crumbled due to age and weather. Beyond the pile of rubble, as they stepped over the rocks, he saw a hole in the wall of the mesa.

"There it is," Laurie said. "Just like I remembered it."

"I thought the cave was in one of those buttes back in the valley," Slocum said.

"There is one there, another cave I mean, but I thought this might be safer for Wallace. It's more remote, and most of the folks in Deadfall have probably never known about it, or have forgotten it."

The three of them stepped inside the cave. They had to hunch over, but once inside, the walls widened and there was a large space that appeared to have been used as a shelter in recent times.

Overhead, there was a feeble light from a hole in the ceiling.

Slocum set down his sack and walked over to where the light sprayed down. He looked up into the hole. In the dimness, he saw blue sky.

"That's odd," he said. "That air hole seems to go clear to the top of the mesa."

"It does," Laurie said. "Whoever started this mine drilled a hole so that he could breathe fresh air. Look at the ground around it. You can see where water has dripped and drained into the soil."

Slocum looked down and saw that there were dry rivulets and furrows in the ground where water had dropped and run over a considerable length of time.

He breathed the air that came down through the hole.

Hornaday set his sack down.

Laurie unslung the canteens and walked over to a small bench and wiped dust from it.

"If you'll open those sacks, I'll help us stack the food behind this bench," she said. "And to christen the cave, I brought something extra for all of us."

Slocum and Hornaday dragged their sacks to the bench and opened them.

In the top of Slocum's bag was a packet.

"I'll take that," Laurie said. She bent down and snatched the oilskin packet from the top of his bag.

Slocum began to remove airtights and beef jerky from

the sack. He laid them on the bench while Laurie walked away.

Hornaday began pulling out the contents of his bag.

He set the items on the unused portion of the bench: peaches, some potatoes, a can of Arbuckle's coffee, dried string beans, a tin of apricots, another of raisins.

"Better stuff here than me'n Harlan had to eat," Hornaday said.

"It all looks good," Slocum said.

Laurie sat on a flat rock that was set among other flat rocks. They all seemed to have been carried into the cave from outside, from another place.

She unwrapped the oilskin packet and pulled out cloth napkins, forks, a paring knife, and spoons. There was also a can opener, which she laid out with the other utensils on one of the flat rocks.

Then she opened a linen towel that had been folded over the foodstuffs.

Slocum smelled the tang of sugar and looked over at her as he set the last item from his sack on the bench.

"Do I smell bear claws?" he said.

Laurie smiled. Even in the darkened cave, Slocum could see that warm pretty smile.

"You do," she said.

"I smell them bear claws, too," Hornaday said. "Makes my stomach churn."

"Well, if you'll look down the back part of this cave, Wallace, you ought to find a big box made into a cabinet. Open the door and you'll find all kinds of cook pans, a skillet, and a coffeepot. Bring me the coffeepot."

"Yes'm. Hot coffee would be a luxury right now," Wallace said.

"John, you'll find wood back near that cabinet and kindling. If you'll make a fire, I'll make us that coffee."

Slocum and Hornaday walked back to the far end of the cave and saw another big tunnel. The light was dim, but Slocum saw the stack of firewood and kindling. Alongside it was a hatchet.

Wallace found the box and opened the door. Someone had made shelves and he saw all the cooking utensils, including a small coffeepot. He brushed away the dust and grit as he walked back into the biggest part of the cave.

Slocum laid down kindling and chunks of firewood cut from cedars and junipers. He made a pyramid of firewood over squaw wood from pines and lit a match. The fire blazed into life, throwing shadows against the wall.

Laurie measured out four heaping tablespoons from the Arbuckle's can and poured them into the pot. Then she added water from one of the large wooden canteens.

She handed the coffeepot to Slocum.

"See if you can find a place for this," she said.

Slocum pushed the pot next to the fire. The smoke rose up through the hole in the cave's ceiling.

"This place will be perfectly safe for you, Wallace. Those piles of rocks outside will hide the entrance. The smoke going up that chimney will be wisps by the time it reaches the top of the mesa. You'll find bedding way back beyond that storage cabinet. It's probably moldy and smelly by now, but it'll do. It can get quite cold here at night."

"You stayed here, Miss Laurie?" Hornaday asked.

"Harve and I stayed one night here, about a year ago. We were hunting antelope."

"Get any?" Wallace asked as the coffeepot began to rumble with the agitated water.

"Nope. Had fun, though. We killed four jackrabbits and a roadrunner."

Wallace and Slocum laughed.

They sat around the flat stones and Laurie handed out

sugared bear claws she had baked herself, strips of fried bacon, and biscuits that had not yet gone hard.

When the coffee was ready, she poured some into three tin cups that lay on the bench with the foodstuffs.

They ate and drank coffee.

When they were finished, Laurie asked Slocum the question that was burning in her mind.

"You could read some of those smoke signals, John. What do they mean?"

"From what I saw, those signals were calling to all the Apaches to gather someplace. Probably a mesa somewhere around here."

"Do you know why?"

Slocum shook his head.

"No, I don't," he said.

Then he fished around in one of his shirt pockets and pulled out a folded piece of paper.

As Wallace and Laurie watched, Slocum unfolded the paper.

It was a wanted flyer.

At the top, there was the legend: $1000.00.

Underneath, the words WANTED FOR MURDER were printed in bold black letters.

And beneath the printing was an artist's rendition of the wanted man. The name beneath it was Junius Collins.

Then followed a brief description of the killer and his victim, one Faron Longley and information on how to contact the sheriff in Dodge City, Kansas.

"Recognize him?" Slocum asked.

Laurie held the paper at a slant so that Wallace could read the flyer and look at the picture.

"Why, that looks just like Orson Canby," Hornaday said.

"Spittin' image," Laurie declared.

"When I got the order for those horses, I did some checking with the local sheriff," Slocum said. "I didn't find an Orson Canby, but I did see that dodger and so I asked whether or not anyone in town had seen such a man."

"And?" Laurie said.

"Seems when Junius Collins left Dodge, he headed west and by the time he got to Kansas City, he had changed his name to Orson Canby. People there remember him because he beat a man half to death. That man had been at the Long Branch in Dodge when Collins murdered one Faron Longley in cold blood."

"Yes, go on," Laurie said.

"I talked to the man in Kansas City. His name was Dennis Walpole. He said he recognized Collins, and Collins beat him up, tried to kill him. Walpole's friends saved him from certain death. But Canby had to leave town in a hurry."

"So you knew who Orson Canby was before you even came here to Deadfall," she said.

"Faron Longley was a friend of mine," Slocum said. "He and I used to trade horses we got in Mexico. He was a good man and a good friend."

"My God, that's an incredible story. So is that why you brought those horses to Canby?"

"Yes. The only reason. Now I've seen the man and I know he's Junius Collins."

"And you want the reward," Wallace said. "Boy, a thousand dollars. That's a heap of money."

"Faron left a widow and a couple of young kids. If I collect that reward, the money will go to Alice, Faron's widow, who still lives in Dodge."

"You're a strange man, John." Hornaday slurped his coffee. "Mighty strange," he said.

"I hate to see a man like Canby get away with murder," Slocum said. "And it doesn't look like he's changed much."

"You got that right, Slocum," Hornaday said.

"If I can," Slocum said, "I want to take Canby back to Dodge in one piece."

"You mean alive," Laurie said.

"Yes. Alive."

Slocum drew a cheroot out of his pocket as Laurie handed the dodger back to him. He folded it and put it back in his pocket.

Then he lit his cheroot and stared at the dying fire for several moments.

"I hope you get him, John," Laurie said, her voice low and full of concern.

Wallace said nothing. He drank his coffee and wondered what he had gotten into with a man like Orson Canby. Men like that had no place in the West or anywhere else. Yet there they were, living secret lives, with blood on their hands.

Such men were evil.

And Wallace Hornaday felt lucky that he was still alive.

13

Johnny Crowell couldn't stand it any longer.

Steve Beck yelled from the jail where he was trapped. He banged on the door with his fists and shouted in a loud voice.

"Hey, somebody! Get me out of here."

He kicked the jail door until the lock rattled.

And he yelled some more.

The cries were muffled, but Johnny heard them every time he walked out in back of the livery stables.

He wondered why no one came to check on Mr. Beck.

While he was in that quandary, Johnny saw the silhouettes of two men at the back door of the stables.

"What you doin' out there, Johnny?" Boze called out. "Beatin' your pud?"

Hack, beside him, laughed.

Johnny ran toward the two men.

"It's not funny," he said.

"What ain't funny?" Boze asked.

"Don't you hear it? That bangin' on the jail door?"

"I hear it, so what?" Hack said. "Man's goin' to hang later today."

"That ain't the prisoner in there," Johnny said.

"Huh?" Hack's face wore a look of puzzlement.

"That's Mr. Beck," Johnny said. "He's locked in there. And yellin' his head off."

Boze walked over to Johnny, grabbed him by the collar, and shook him.

"What's Beck doin' in jail?" he demanded.

Hack stepped out of the stables and walked up to Boze and Johnny.

"That feller locked him there," Johnny blurted out.

"What feller?" Hack asked.

"You know, the one who sold Canby those horses. Slocum."

"What?" Boze exclaimed.

"Slocum locked up Beck," Hack said. "What happened to Hornaday?"

"Slocum took him. Walked away with him," Johnny said.

"Shit," Boze said.

"Damn him." Hack's face reddened with anger.

"We'll catch hell from Canby over this," Boze said.

"We gotta tell him."

"Where'd Slocum go?" Boze asked.

Johnny shrugged as Boze took his hands away from the young man's collar.

"I don't know."

"Damn you, Johnny," Boze said. "You should have told somebody."

"That's a jailbreak," Hack said. "A criminal offense."

"We oughta hang this squirt of water for not tellin' anyone," Boze said.

Johnny shrank away, suddenly fearful.

"I—I didn't know who to tell. For all I knew, it was a joke," Johnny said.

"A joke?" Boze snapped.

"Man takes a prisoner out of jail and locks his guard inside. What's funny about that?" Hack said.

"I don't know," Johnny said.

"Get your ass down the street. You find Canby. Tell him what happened," Boze said.

"Yes sir," Johnny said.

"Let's see if we can find the key to that jail lock," Boze said to Hack as Crowell scampered through the stables at a run.

"Damn that Slocum," Hack said.

"Damn that kid, Johnny," Boze said.

The two walked out of the livery and turned the corner to the back street.

They could hear Beck hollering as they approached the jail.

His voice was getting hoarse. They heard him kick the door and then it was silent.

The two gunmen walked up to the jail door. Hack shook the lock.

"Beck?" Boze said in a loud voice.

"That you, Bozeman?"

"Yeah. You got the key to this lock?"

"Hell no. Get me out of here, Boze."

Beck's voice was weak. He stood close to the door. He leaned against it for support.

"Slocum took my scattergun and pistol, too. Look over by the bench. I heard a clanking sound after he locked me in here."

"Keep your pants on, Steve," Boze said. "We'll have a look."

The door creaked as Beck leaned against it in despair.

The two men walked around to the side. They saw the bench.

Underneath it they saw Beck's shotgun and his pistol. There were cartridges on the ground—.36 caliber.

"Look around for a key," Boze said.

"I *am* looking," Hack said. "So far, no sign of it."

"The bastard probably took it with him," Boze said.

"More'n likely, the son of a bitch."

The two men scoured the ground all around the bench. No key.

Hack threw up his arms.

"Nary a sign of that key," he said.

"Wonder if we should break the damned lock," Boze said.

"There's probably only one key. That lock's older'n Methuselah."

"Yeah," Boze said.

They left shotgun, pistol, and cartridges where they lay and walked back to the jail door.

"You find the key?" Beck called out.

"No, we didn't," Boze said. "Is there another key somewhere?"

"I—I don't think so," Beck said. "You got to get me out of here. It stinks from Hornaday's shit and piss."

"We'll have to break the lock, Steve," Hack said.

"Break it, then," Beck said. "We can always get another damned lock."

"Hold on," Boze said. "We got to find a crowbar or a hammer."

"Look in the livery," Beck said. His voice had grown weaker. The door creaked as he stood away from it.

"Go find something, Hack," Boze said.

"Hurry," Beck said, his voice down to a whine.

"Shit," Hack said.

He walked away, headed for the corner. Boze leaned against the jail wall again.

"He'll find something, Steve," he said. He pulled the makings from his pocket and began to roll a cigarette. "We'll get you out of there pronto."

"Pronto can't be too soon," Beck said. "I'm suffocatin' in here."

"Won't be long," Boze said. He licked the paper to seal it around the tobacco. He stuck the cigarette in his mouth and lit it. The sun was bearing down on him and he had begun to sweat.

It must be near noon, he thought. Hornaday had been due to hang around three that afternoon.

Now, he was gone and Slocum had him.

Where?

Where in hell could a man go in Deadfall? With a prisoner at that?

Bozeman puzzled over those questions until he saw Hackberry round the corner, a crowbar in his left hand. He seemed in no hurry.

"Get your ass over here, Hack. Man's dyin' in that hoosegow."

Hack did not quicken his pace.

"Keep your shirt on, Boze. I'm all out of hurry after lookin' for this here crowbar."

Beck whined behind the jail door.

Boze grabbed the crowbar out of Hack's hand and tossed his cigarette down. He ground it into the dirt with the heel of his boot.

Boze slid the straight end of the crowbar into the loop of the lock.

When it was solid, he pushed hard, down, and to one side.

He grunted.

The lock snapped open with a crack.

Boze slipped the lock from the hasp and opened the door.

Beck staggered out.

The stench from inside the jail wafted outside after him.

"Thank God, Boze. You got me out."

"Your weapons are back by your bench, Steve. Pull yourself together," Boze said.

Beck's face was grimy and drenched with his sour sweat. His shirt was soaked through and his hands oily.

Beck hurried around to the side of the jail as Hack and Boze waited for him.

When he returned, he was carrying his shotgun and loading cartridges into the cylinder of the LeMat. It was awkward, juggling the shotgun and trying to stuff fresh cartridges into his pistol.

"What the hell happened, Steve?" Boze asked as Beck came close. Beck finished loading his pistol and stuffed it into its holster.

"I was a-settin' out there on my bench, when this feller come up to me," he said. "He wore all back duds. He was a tall one."

"Yeah, we know. What did he say?" Hack asked.

"Not much. He grabbed my scattergun and threatened me. He took my key and walked me around to the jail. He unlocked it and shoved me inside, took Hornaday out. Then he locked me in."

"You dumb bastard," Boze said. "You were supposed to guard the prisoner, keep him locked up."

"That feller jumped me, I tell you. Came out of nowhere. One minute I was a-settin' there, and next, he's right there. Menacing he was. Downright menacing."

"I'll menace you, Beck, if you don't calm down and tell the whole story," Beck said.

"That is the whole story."

"Any idea where Slocum took Hornaday?"

"Yeah, that was his name, Slocum. He told me like he didn't care who knowed who it was that broke Hornaday out of jail."

"Did he say anything to Hornaday? Like where he was takin' him?" Hack asked.

Beck shook his head.

"No. Like I said, he didn't say much. I heard him walk around and throw my guns down, then the footsteps just faded away."

"Well, he's somewhere," Hack said.

Boze looked at his partner as if he had gone daft.

"Well, yeah, Hack, Slocum and Hornaday are sure as hell somewhere. But where?"

"Damned if I know," Hack said.

"We got to find them, or Canby will tack our hides to the barn and set the barn on fire," Boze said.

"Where do we look?" Hack asked. "In town? The saloon? Hotel?"

"No, you dumb bastard. Saloon ain't open yet and Slocum damned sure wouldn't check into the hotel with a jail-broke prisoner. Unless he's stupid, like you."

"Get off my ass, Boze," Hack said. "I was just feelin' my way about where they might have gone."

"Well, we ain't goin' to waste time lookin' where you think they ought to be."

"Maybe they saddled up and rode out," Hack said. "Lit a shuck for Flagstaff or Phoenix."

Beck continued to sweat.

"I didn't hear no horses ridin' away," he said. "Far as I know, Slocum come up here on foot."

"We'll see if that black horse of his is still in the livery," Boze said.

Then he looked at Beck.

"What are you going to do, Steve?"

"I got to tell Orson what happened. He'll be mad as hell, but I got to tell him."

"I hope you got prayers enough to cover it, Steve," Boze said. "Mad ain't the word for what Orson's goin' to be when he finds out about this."

"He probably already knows," Hack said. "Johnny's probably told him about the jailbreak by now."

Beck's face drained of color.

Boze felt sorry for the little man. Hell, he might have done the same thing if Slocum had come up on him suddenlike. Out of nowhere.

He patted Beck on the shoulder.

"Just tell Orson what happened, Steve. He likely won't blame you as much as he'll blame us. We let Slocum out of our sight when we were supposed to be watchin' him."

"You think so?" Beck said.

Boze didn't have the heart to tell Beck no. He didn't think Orson would understand. He'd just blame.

And he and Hack were bound to get a lashing as well.

Or worse.

14

On the long walk back to Laurie's cabin, they stopped to talk to Harvey again.

As they walked up to his mine, Harvey pushed a wheelbarrow over to a small pile of rocks and dumped the rocks in the wheelbarrow into the pile. He was soaked with sweat and wiped his face with a bandanna, then stuffed it in his back pocket.

"Everything work out with Wallace?" he said, his words slowed by his panting breath.

"Safe and sound," Laurie said.

"Good," Harvey said.

He looked at Slocum with admiring eyes. He was still astonished that he had finally met the man who had impressed him back in Abilene.

"We're going to the cabin," Laurie said. "See you later?"

"Maybe," Harvey said. "I want to finish my own cabin. I've got the roof on and a few more logs came in yesterday from Flagstaff. Just have a few things to do."

"You're building your own cabin?" Slocum asked.

"Started it two months ago. Just a few more logs and it'll be finished. I'll be staying there from now on, sis."

"Have everything you need, Harve?"

"Yep. Got the stove all set up. Good chimney. Food stocked in the cupboards I planed the other day. All set."

"I'll miss your company, Harve."

"I won't be far away. Just holler, sis, if you need me."

"Where is your cabin?" Slocum asked.

"About five hundred yards from where Laurie's is. It's a little behind hers, up against the butte. In fact, my back wall is the butte itself. Saved me some lumber."

"I'd like to see it sometime," Slocum said.

"I'll take you there tomorrow maybe."

"See you, Harve," Laurie said.

As she and Slocum turned to walk away, Harvey called to them. They both halted and faced him.

"I saw something odd yesterday when that wagon pulled into town with my logs," Harvey said.

"Oh?" Laurie's head snapped back as she eyed her brother.

"There was another supply wagon from Flagstaff that pulled up," Harvey said. "I couldn't help but notice what was in it."

"Tell us," Laurie said.

"Rifles," he said. "Carbines. Spencers. And boxes of ammunition. Enough for a small army."

"That's odd," Laurie said.

Slocum's interest perked up.

Why, he wondered, would someone haul in army carbines and ammunition? There was no army in Deadfall. No fort within miles of the settlement. And who were the guns for?

"How many rifles would you say were in that shipment?" Slocum asked.

"There were ten rifles in each box and I counted ten boxes. There were about twenty boxes of cartridges. I saw U.S. ARMY stamped on all the boxes."

"Stolen?" Slocum said.

Harvey shrugged. "Maybe," he said. "I wondered about it. Two of Canby's men covered up the wagon with a heavy tarp and two more men came and drove it around in back of the hotel."

"Hmm," Slocum murmured.

"What can it mean?" Laurie asked.

"I'd be curious to know if that wagon is still parked behind the hotel. I'll add that to my list of things to do tonight."

Both Harvey and Laurie looked hard at Slocum. His face was a mask, divulging not a trace of his thoughts.

"What are you going to do tonight?" Laurie asked.

"I want Canby," he said. "But from what I've seen, he's like the heart of an artichoke."

"What do you mean, John?" Laurie asked.

"You have to peel away all the leaves to get to the heart. Canby is surrounded by gunmen."

"So? What do you plan to do, John?" Harvey asked.

"Peel away those leaves, Harvey," Slocum said. "One by one until only Canby is left."

"You mean kill all his men?" Harvey said.

"If necessary," Slocum said.

Laurie shuddered as if from a sudden chill.

"You mean," she said, "in cold blood?"

"I'm not going to backshoot any of them if that's what you're driving at," he said.

"From what I saw in Abilene, sis, Slocum meets his enemies face to face. He's not a backshooter."

"I didn't mean that," she said. "I just wondered if you were going to shoot his men down, one by one."

"We'll see," Slocum said.

"How?" she asked.

"They'll have a choice," Slocum said.

"What kind of choice?" Laurie said, visibly upset at the thought of Slocum as a gunman who would shoot and kill men, for whatever reasons.

"Whether they want to live or die," Slocum said, and he looked at the sky. There were no more puffs of smoke, only a blue expanse devoid of clouds.

Then he looked at Laurie and smiled.

She shuddered again and looked away.

Harvey stood there as if struck dumb. He remembered Slocum in Abilene. Calm, cool, deliberate in the face of death.

He hadn't backed down then, and Harvey was sure Slocum was more than a match for Canby's men.

But he was badly outnumbered.

There was no telling how many men Canby had under his command. Slocum was facing a tough and ruthless enemy. And there was not a man who worked for Canby who would hesitate to shoot Slocum in the back.

Slocum might not even see the man who raised a gun against him.

"Is Canby that important, John?" Harvey asked. "Shouldn't you let the law take care of him? Why risk your own life?"

"There seems to be no law here," Slocum said. "Canby's already shown his true colors by framing an innocent man and hanging him. And he was about to hang another innocent man, Wallace Hornaday."

"But you're not the law, John," Laurie said.

"Where there is no law," Slocum said, "it's sometimes up to the law-abiding to take the law into their own hands."

"Nobody's stood up to Canby here in Deadfall," Harvey said. "Even I would hesitate to buck him."

"Not every law-abiding citizen can combat evil," Slocum said.

"But you appoint yourself as judge, jury, and executioner," Laurie said, plainly upset.

"I wouldn't say that," Slocum said.

"What would you say, then?" Harvey asked.

"When I see a town like Deadfall, with no law and a tyrant running things, it angers me," Slocum said.

"That's still no excuse to start killing," Laurie said.

"Some people are rabbits," Slocum said. "When there's danger, they freeze or hide."

"And you, what are you, John?"

"Maybe a wolf," he said with a slow curl of his lips into a half smile.

"Well, Canby's a wolf, too, then," Laurie said. "And you would descend to his level."

"There are good wolves and bad wolves," Slocum said, the smile widening.

"Oh, you men," Laurie said. "You just do what you want to do and to hell with everyone else."

"I said I'd give Canby's men a chance," Slocum said. "And if it's possible, I want to capture Canby alive and take him back to Dodge to face justice."

"All very noble and admirable," Laurie said, still upset. "And you might get yourself killed."

"And if I don't face off with these men," Slocum said, "more innocent men might die here."

Laurie clamped her mouth shut to keep from protesting further.

Harvey looked at Slocum with fresh eyes.

"He makes a point, sis. I wish I could stand up to Canby for what he did to Harlan and what he was about to do to Wallace."

He looked apologetically at Slocum.

Laurie drew in a deep breath and brushed her hair away from her face with the back of her hand.

"I—I don't know what to say," she said.

Slocum gave her a moment to compose herself.

"Sometimes," he said, "you can't sweep a problem under the rug. As long as Deadfall tolerates such a man as Canby, he'll take more and more from them. The best way to solve a problem is to face it head on. Win or lose."

"You might lose, John," she said. "I would hate to see that."

"She's right, John," Harvey said. "You're taking on a dangerous task to go up against any one of the men who work for Canby. And there's several of them."

"We'll just have to see how it all works out," Slocum said.

"You sound sure of yourself," Harvey said.

"But he doesn't know how dangerous Canby is," she said.

"Time will tell," Slocum said and turned to walk away.

Laurie ran after him. She grabbed him by the sleeve and tugged at his arm.

"Will you promise me one thing, John?" she said.

"If I can," he said.

"Stay with me tonight."

"I'm going hunting tonight," he said.

"So long," Harvey called. "Take care, John."

Laurie and Slocum turned and waved good-bye to Harvey.

He waved back.

"After you're through hunting," she said as they continued to walk along the creek, "just promise me you'll come back to my cabin. I'll leave the door unlocked."

"It would be a pleasure," he said. She leaned close to him and he smelled the perfume in her hair.

"If I come back," he said.

She squeezed his arm and her touch felt good to him.

He didn't know how far he would get with his mission that night, but he was going to try and confront as many of Canby's men as he could.

And he wanted to check on the two women, Bonnie and Renata. If his hunch was right, they were already in Canby's clutches.

That was one more item on Slocum's list.

15

Orson Canby sat in a large chair in the center of his hotel suite.

To Johnny Crowell, who was shaking in his boots, he looked like a bloated bullfrog on a lily pad.

Hack and Boze flanked Steve Beck on the large plush couch made of Moroccan leather. Johnny had heard it all from Beck, as had Canby, and now he knew the whole story of the jailbreak.

Beck was on the hot seat, Johnny knew. Canby's criticism of the jailer was scathing.

"You little twerp," Canby said to Beck. "You are paid to guard prisoners. You let yourself be bushwhacked by this Slocum bastard. Can you give me one good reason why you shouldn't be thrashed for your dereliction?"

"Boss, that Slocum feller caught me by surprise. He was on me before I could do anything. He grabbed my scattergun and I thought he was goin' to shoot me dead."

"Beck, you make me want to puke," Canby said.

There was a knock at the door.

"Come in," Canby said in a loud tone of voice.

Two men entered the living quarters.

Both seemed out of breath.

Roddie Nehring and Earl Cassaway clumped across the rug. Canby waved them to single chairs near the divan.

"He ain't left town," Earl said.

"Leastways, his horse is still in a stall at the livery," Roddie said as both men sat down.

"This is a fine kettle of fish," Canby said as he looked at his four henchmen.

"He just don't seem to be nowhere," Hack ventured.

"Shut up, Hack," Canby said.

Orson rubbed four fingers and his thumb, bringing them together on his forehead as if he were summoning thought and, perhaps, wisdom.

"Sorry," Hack said, then clamped his mouth shut.

"Well, he's somewhere," Canby said. "And you're all out of ideas. And he's got that bastard Hornaday with him. Hornaday's due to be hanged, and by God, he's going to hang. Slocum, too, if we can find him. Jailbreaking is a crime no matter where it happens. That right, Beck?"

Beck appeared flustered.

"If you say so, Orson," Beck said.

"Well, here's what you're going to do, boys, and you pass the word along to Rodrigo and Salazar. You cover both ends of Main Street this afternoon. One man at each corner. Got that?"

The four gunmen nodded.

"Hack, you get Rodrigo on one corner. I want you to find a dark corner in the Wild Horse and sit there until it closes. Don't get drunk. Just sit there like you was a stump."

"Got it, Orson," Hack said.

"Bose, you put Salazar on a corner opposite Rodrigo

and you prowl Main Street. Check Mrs. Hobbs's boardinghouse every so often, and the hotel here. Slocum's got to light somewhere."

Boze squirmed on the divan.

"Orson. Maybe Slocum took Hornaday out of town on foot."

"His saddlebags and rifles ain't in the livery," Earl said. "His saddle and bridle are there."

"I'm damned tired of hearing where Slocum and Hornaday ain't," Orson said. "Find them."

"You want 'em alive, or do we shoot them?" Hack asked.

"Shoot 'em if you have to, but if you can wrestle 'em down and hog-tie 'em, I'd like to see their necks stretched on the gallows," Orson said.

The four gunmen left the room, leaving only Steve Beck and Johnny Crowell still there.

"Johnny," Orson said, "go on back to your job at the livery."

"Sure, boss," Johnny said and walked quickly out the door.

"Steve, I got a little job for you," Orson said.

"Yes, sir."

"I want you to find Ruben Machado for me. You know where he lives?"

"Sure do, Orson," Beck said.

"Tell him to hightail it over here quick as possible. You got that?"

Beck rose from his seat and donned his hat.

"I'll get him here, Orson."

"Then you better buy another lock for that jail. With your own money."

"Yes, sir, I'll do that, too."

"Get a good one this time," Orson said.

Beck left the hotel room and Orson rose from his chair and walked to the window. He paced back and forth, glancing at the face of a butte some distance away.

Less than a half hour later, there was a knock at his door.

"Come in," he said, and turned to walk back to his chair.

He stood behind the big chair as the door opened and Ruben Machado walked in, his stubble-flocked face shadowed by the brim of his dark hat.

Orson sat down.

"Come on in, Ruben," he said.

Ruben took off his hat and walked over to where Orson sat.

"You ready, Ruben?" Orson said.

"I am ready," Ruben said, half bowing to emphasize his obedience to Canby.

"Tomorrow, you and Paco haul that wagon out to Sunrise Mesa. You know where it is?"

"I do," Ruben said.

"When you deliver the guns, you tell Chief Blue Wolf to wait for my order."

"Your order?" Ruben said.

"He will know what I mean, Ruben. You just tell him that."

"What do we do after we deliver the guns to Blue Wolf?" Ruben asked.

"You and Paco come back here, drive the wagon to the middle of Gravel Gulch, and leave it there. Then, you boys put up the draft horses, saddle up, and hightail it for Tucson."

"Yes," Ruben said.

"I will meet you there in a few days with more money. Got that?"

"Yes, Paco and I will do what you say, Orson," Ruben said.

"On your way out, stop by Mr. Jennings's office and tell him I want to see him right away."

"Tomorrow, we go," Ruben said.

"Perfect, Ruben. *Vaya con Dios*."

Ruben bowed, put his hat back on, and hurried from the room.

Orson listened for his footsteps out in the hall. Matt Jennings was his accountant and had an office on the mezzanine of the hotel.

Orson waited for him, a fresh cigar in his mouth. He reached for a match on a nearby end table and picked up the box.

By the time he'd trimmed the end of the cigar and lit it, Jennings came through the door.

Jennings never knocked when Orson sent for him. He carried a ledger in one hand and a pencil and tablet in the other.

"Sit down, Matt," Orson said. "At the table there."

"You're in a bright mood, Orson," Jennings said.

"I got my reasons," Orson said.

Jennings sat down at the round table inset with various wood designs. He set down the ledger and opened the tablet. He positioned the pencil over the tablet and seemed prepared to write.

"I see you brought the books, Matt," Orson said.

"Yes. In case you wanted to go over the figures."

Jennings did not smile. He was all business.

"And how are we doing?" Orson asked.

"Very well, Orson," Jennings said. "And if you take over that mine once owned by Devlin and Hornaday, I expect you'll do even better. The assay was quite favorable."

"I know," Orson said. "Richest mine so far. But soon, we'll have all the mines here in Deadfall."

Orson puffed on his cigar, and let the smoke leak out of the sides of his mouth.

"Oh?" Jennings said. "How will that come to be, and why all the mines?"

"By week's end, you and I will be on our way to Tucson. A band of Apaches will raze this damned town to ashes and kill everyone in it."

"That seems rather drastic," Jennings said. "Wholesale murder, in fact."

"Can't be helped. I knew this day would come and now it's here."

"What day is that, Orson?" Jennings asked.

"The day my past catches up with me. A man came into town this morning with some horses I bought from him. He broke Hornaday out of jail this morning. That got me to thinking."

"Got you to thinking, Orson? About what?"

"About Dodge City," Orson said.

Jennings's face turned pale as it drained of blood.

He seemed to choke to get the words out.

"I—I thought that was behind us, Orson. For good."

"The man who sold me the horses," Orson said. "His name is Slocum."

"John Slocum?" Jennings sputtered. Spittle flew onto his string tie and his pressed blue shirt. Jennings was clean-shaven with dark brown hair and blue-gray eyes, a thin neck, and thin arms and legs. He wore a pinstripe suit and wing-tip shoes. He wore no hat and Orson envied him his thick curly hair.

"The same, Matt," Orson said.

"Jesus Christ," Jennings said. "He was a friend of Faron Longley's, I recall, and people in Dodge warned us that Slocum would be on your tail."

"Slocum will be dead by sunrise," Orson said.

"You sure, Orson?"

Jennings fidgeted with his string tie, flipping one strand

over the other. He was visibly nervous, and his fingers all trembled.

"There's no way out for him," Orson said. "I've got men all over town looking for him. And if he slips out of this trap, in a few days he'll be burned to a crisp by the Apaches."

"You think of everything, Orson," Jennings said.

"We'll have to change our names again, but we'll be back in Deadfall to reap the rewards. Mining claims, miners working for us. The whole shebang."

Jennings let out a low whistle.

"You think of just about everything, Orson," Jennings said. "I'm glad we're on the same side."

"You've been faithful to me ever since I plugged Longley, Matt," Orson said. "I believe in rewarding my closest friends."

"When do we leave town?" Jennings asked.

"About four days from now, five at the most. Everything's set."

"What's the signal for Blue Wolf?" Jennings asked. He knew about the Apaches and how Orson had bribed them with guns and whiskey since coming to Deadfall.

"There'll be an empty wagon right smack in the middle of the valley," Orson said. "I'll set it on fire and the smoke will bring the Apaches down on Deadfall within an hour or two."

"Christ," Jennings said.

"Too bad we won't be here to watch it, Matt."

Jennings swiped a hand across his sweaty forehead.

"I don't want to see it," he said.

"It'll be pure hell for everybody here," Orson said.

He pulled smoke from his cigar and smiled through a blue haze as he let it out.

Jennings sat there, half-dazed at the magnitude of Orson's plan.

He had known Collins was a ruthless man back in Dodge City, but had never dreamed the man could be as heartless and savage as the Apaches.

He vowed then and there never to cross Orson.

Orson wouldn't even blink if he meant to murder him, Jennings knew.

"I'll have everything ready to go when you tell me," Jennings said. "Cash, gold, the books."

"Be ready in three days, Matt," Orson said.

"I hope you get Slocum," Jennings said. "He's a most dangerous man."

"I know," Orson said. "But at bottom he's no different than any other man. He'll bleed just as much."

The smoke rose in the air and hung suspended until it began to drift into nothingness.

Just like the silence as both men thought about the horror that was soon to happen in Deadfall.

16

Marlene Vanders watched the two girls walk by her table at the Wild Horse Saloon. Bonnie and Renata were dressed in new outfits sewn by Maria and Teresa, who sat with her.

"You've got to sway your hips more, Renata," Marlene said.

"Huh?" Renata stopped in her tracks and looked at Marlene.

"You're too stiff, honey," Marlene said.

"I don't see why I have to walk a certain way," Renata said.

Bonnie whispered something to her.

Renata turned to look at Marlene.

"I've had men attracted to me without my having to display my bare legs," Renata said to Marlene.

"Tonight this room will be filled with men who are smoking, playing cards, drinking. They want to look at pretty women and that's why you have to show your feminine side, dearie."

Bonnie smiled and walked around. She swayed her hips.

"Like that," Marlene said.

Maria and Teresa tittered.

Just then, Carrie Hobbs came in through the batwing doors. She walked over to the table where Marlene and her two girls were sitting.

"Did you hear the news?" she asked, not bothering to lower her voice.

Carrie was a matronly forty-five or so, with her graying hair tied up in a bun, her seersucker dress covered by a polka-dotted apron. She wore low-heeled shoes. Her face resembled a wrinkled pudding, while her eyes were porcine and sunken, close-set beside a large hooked nose.

"What news?"

"Men just searched my boardinghouse looking for that prisoner, Hornaday. They said he broke out of jail this mornin'."

"No, I hadn't heard."

Renata and Bonnie sidled over to the table.

"Did you say Hornaday?" Bonnie asked Mrs. Hobbs.

"Yes, Wallace Hornaday, a horse thief."

"He was the man I was supposed to marry," Bonnie said.

"Well, don't get your hopes up, girlie," Carrie said. "If they don't shoot Wallace on sight, they'll surely hang him."

"How'd he break out of jail?" Marlene asked.

"They say a man named Slocum broke him out. They're lookin' for him, too."

"Slocum?" Bonnie blurted out. "John Slocum? Renata and I know him."

"Well, he's a wanted man now," Carrie said.

Bonnie and Renata looked stricken.

"Who is this Slocum anyway?" Marlene asked. "I never heard of him."

Teresa and Maria came to life next to Marlene. They giggled.

"What is it?" Marlene asked them.

"Slocum is a big man," Maria said. "Came here with Obie and those two girls. Obie said he bedded them before they got here."

"You slept with this Slocum?" Marlene asked the two new girls.

"I'll never tell," Bonnie said.

Renata blushed.

"You should see him, Marlene," Bonnie said. "You'd want him, too."

Marlene drew herself up.

"There's no man here in Deadfall that I would ever want," she said.

"You two look very pretty in those outfits," Carrie said to Bonnie and Renata.

They were wearing white satin bodices with black vertical stripes, short black skirts, mesh stockings with red garters, and high-heeled shoes spangled with silver bows.

"Thank you, Mrs. Hobbs," Bonnie said.

Renata curtsied and smiled.

"Well, I've lost two boarders," Carrie said, "but lunch will be ready when you're all through here. Have the girls seen their rooms upstairs yet?"

"Not yet," Marlene said. "We'll do that now and then come over for lunch."

"Very well," Carrie said. She turned on her heel and walked out of the saloon.

"Aren't we staying with Mrs. Hobbs anymore?" Renata asked.

"Why no, Renata," Marlene said. "See those rooms up on the balcony? Those are your new quarters."

"Oh," Bonnie said.

Marlene looked at Maria and Teresa.

"Bring their clothes over from Carrie's," she told them. "You did a fine job on their clothes. Make another set before tomorrow."

The two Mexican women nodded and got up from the table. Teresa picked up a small wicker basket with pieces of cloth and sewing materials, and the two walked out through the batwing doors.

"Follow me, gals," Marlene said, and rose from the table.

She took the two upstairs to the balcony and opened one door, then went to the next and opened it.

"These will be your rooms while you work for me," she said.

"They're so small," Bonnie said.

"Tiny," Renata said.

"You'll eat at Mrs. Hobbs's boardinghouse, but sleep here at night. This is also where you'll entertain your guests."

Each room had a small brass bed, a table and chairs, a small divan, and a sideboard with water, glasses, a pitcher, and a comb and brush. There was a bedpan under each bed and several towels on hooks.

"Entertain?" Renata asked.

"Guests," Marlene said. "Pick which room you want. Maria will fetch your clothes from Carrie Hobbs."

"I—I don't know about this," Renata said.

"You'll learn, sweetie," Marlene said. She closed both doors and the three of them left the saloon to walk next door to Mrs. Hobbs's boardinghouse.

Outside the boardinghouse, they met up with Hack and Boze, who were just leaving.

"Marlene, we're going to check the Wild Horse for an escaped prisoner," Hack said as he touched a finger to the brim of his hat in greeting.

"You won't find any jailbirds there," she said.

"Have you seen a tall man wearin' black clothes?" Boze asked.

"Slocum, you mean?" Marlene said. "No, I haven't. Stay away from the bar when you go over there, boys. I keep track of my liquor."

"Oh, we wouldn't touch any of your bottles," Hack said. "Orson would raise hell."

"And so would I," Marlene said.

The two men looked at the skimpily clad girls and their eyes widened.

They walked on to the saloon next door while Marlene and her charges entered the boardinghouse to the aroma of biscuits, pot roast, steamed spinach, and other foods prepared by Carrie's cook.

"I hope Slocum gets away," Renata whispered to Bonnie as they entered the dining room.

"I hope Mr. Hornaday gets away, too," Bonnie said.

"You still going to marry him?" Renata asked.

"I sure hope so."

"I'd like to marry Slocum," Renata said.

Marlene gave both girls a sharp look.

"You're a dreamer, Renata," Bonnie said.

"That's what I've been doin' all my life," Renata replied.

Marlene snorted in disapproval.

17

Laurie led Slocum to her brother's nearly completed cabin. He had transplanted cactus and juniper trees to partially conceal the building and to add a touch of beauty to his digs.

"Harve put a lot of work into his cabin, and mine," she said.

Slocum saw the pile of pine logs set to one side, but could see that Harvey had not yet finished debarking all of them.

"He does fine work," he said.

"He's going to transplant some cactus and trees around my cabin when he gets time," she said.

"A lot of work," Slocum said.

The two walked to Laurie's cabin, which was taking the brunt of the afternoon sun as it traversed its westward path across the skies.

Inside, though, it was relatively cool as Slocum would have expected. Logs made for good insulation in both summer and winter.

"I'll show you Harve's room, where you can stay until it's safe for you to leave," she said.

Slocum followed her down the hall. She opened a door and went inside.

"All the comforts of home," she said.

The room was large with a small brass bed, straight chairs, a small desk and table, three lamps, a window with a view of the valley, and another door that amounted to a private entrance from the side of the cabin.

"Pretty nice," Slocum said. "What do you charge for a night's stay?"

Laurie laughed and grabbed his arm.

"You might as well see the rest of the cabin," she said.

She led him back into the hall and opened another door on the opposite side. This room was bigger than the other. It had a large four-poster bed with a canopy, an overstuffed chair, a small desk next to the wall, a leaf table, and straight-back chairs. There were framed Currier & Ives prints on the walls. No side or back door, and the view from the back window was of the creek and the butte several yards away.

"Even nicer," Slocum said.

"It's quiet and peaceful. Come on, I'll show you the kitchen and we have a privy out back."

The kitchen was large with lots of cabinet and counter space. There was a woodstove and utensils hanging from a roof beam. There was even a clothes tree by the back door and several wooden pegs driven into the log walls.

The kitchen smelled of sage and flour, of coffee and sugar. There was a coffeepot on the cold stove and a wooden tray on the counter with side handles.

"You must love to cook," he said.

Laurie laughed.

"Harvey loves to eat. And so do I. I'll fix us a nice supper."

They walked back to the front room. Slocum sat in the easy chair, while Laurie seated herself on the divan.

"I'm still trying to absorb and understand all the information I got from you today, John."

"You mean the smoke signals?"

"No, the Canby stuff. It's hard to believe the man has come this far and is wanted by the law."

"He murdered my friend over a business deal," Slocum said. "He wasn't satisfied with the money he made and wanted it all for himself."

"So he's ruthless," Laurie said.

"Yes, he is that. In spades."

"What are you going to do? How will you ever capture such a man? He's evaded the law this long. He'll be hard to catch or to bring down."

"Yes, I expect that's so," Slocum said. He patted his shirt with a hand.

"Missing something?" she said.

"A cheroot. I have more in my saddlebags."

He got up and walked to where Laurie had placed his saddlebags and rifle. He opened one pouch and grabbed up several cigars from a tin, stuck them into his pocket.

"May I smoke?" he said as he sat back down.

"Sure. That's Harvey's pipe next to the ashtray on the end table there."

Slocum looked over and saw the pipe and ashtray. The pipe bowl was hard-baked clay and the stem carved from hickory or ash. He pulled a cheroot from his pocket and lit it with a wooden match he struck on the heel of his boot. He blew the smoke away from where Laurie was sitting.

"Tonight," he said, "I'll slip into town and see what I can find out."

"What do you mean? What are you trying to find out?"

Laurie crossed her legs and he could see her ankles above her lace-up boots.

"By now, Canby probably knows about the jailbreak. He'll have men looking for me. I want to see what he's up to by way of finding me."

"Won't that be risky?" she asked.

"Living is risky," he said.

"I mean dangerous. What if they see you?"

"There are no streetlamps in Deadfall," he said. "I wear dark clothes. I can see if men with rifles are watching for me and Hornaday. I've seen some of the men's faces who work for him."

"Sounds to me as if you are expecting trouble, John. Gunplay maybe?"

He smiled and pulled smoke into his mouth and lungs. He let the smoke out slowly and leaned back in the chair.

"I am going to be very quiet while I prowl through town," he said.

Laurie cocked her head and gave him a skeptical look.

"Like a cat?" she said.

"Like a cougar."

"Still, if some of his men see you, they might open fire on you. With pistols or rifles. Maybe both."

"They might," he said. "I can't read Canby's mind, but I imagine he's given orders to his men."

"What orders?"

"Shoot on sight," he said. "Shoot to kill."

"And what orders do you give yourself, John?"

He looked out the front window, down the long valley.

"The same," he said, "with reservations and conditions."

"Now that's not very straight talk, John. What reservations? What restrictions?"

"I always give a man the chance to back down, to think it over if he plans to draw down on me."

"It'll be dark. You're wearing dark clothes, as you say,

and you're tall. You'd be unmistakable against the men who work for Orson Canby."

"I'll be small tonight," he said and smiled.

"Oh, you. You'll probably just shoot anybody you see who looks suspicious. Harvey said you were a fast draw and had deadly aim with a six-gun. There are not many men who can shoot that well, he told me."

"I have a lot of practice with a six-shooter," he said. "I'll still give a man a chance to think about living or dying."

She was silent for several moments while Slocum smoked. He tapped the cheroot over the ashtray to drop the ash.

"I'll worry about you tonight," she said.

"No need to worry."

"You don't know how vicious Canby's men are. How sneaky."

"I have a pretty good idea," he said.

She uncrossed her legs and Slocum admired the clean lines of her body, the flare of her hips, her delicate throat, her beautiful patrician face. She was a beautiful woman and wise in the ways of men. He wondered how far she would take him if they ever drew close.

It was not something he would pursue on such a slender thread of friendship, but the desire was there. At least it was in him. He did not know about Laurie. She was, like many beautiful and smart women, mysterious and elusive.

Not yet, he told himself. Just wait.

They spent the afternoon talking as he smoked, and when the sun began to set, Laurie arose from her chair and went to the kitchen.

"Just enjoy the evening," she said. "I'll call you when supper's ready."

He nodded and looked at the dining area a few feet from the front room.

He heard her as she set out plates and eating utensils, the clank of pots and pans from the kitchen. He carried his bedroll, saddlebags, and rifle to the room that had been Harvey's and set them on the table. There was a space to hang clothing and store his saddlebags. He laid his bedroll on the bed and punched one of the pillows. It was soft and his fist impression disappeared as it resumed its shape.

They ate at the dining room table. The sun sank below the end of the valley, and all the long shadows congealed into a single dark patch. The light lingered on the rims of the buttes for a long while as they forked pork and boiled new potatoes into their mouths, speared string beans, and spooned up apricots and pitted olives.

"I would have baked a pie if I had known I'd have a guest in my home," she said.

"I haven't had pie in six months," he said.

Laurie laughed.

"Maybe I'll bake one for you tomorrow," she said.

Neither of them wanted to mention that there might not be a tomorrow. At least for one of them.

"Coffee?"

"Might perk me up," he said. "Sure."

She carried cups, saucers, and the coffeepot on the tray he had seen in the kitchen. She set it on the dining table and poured steaming coffee into their cups. Then she handed a cup and saucer across the table to Slocum.

"We can drink these in the front room if you like," she said.

They both got up and took their coffee with them. Slocum savored the aroma of Arbuckle's with its slight cinnamon tang before he drank the first sip.

Later, when it was full dark, he got up and looked down at Laurie. She looked sleepy.

"I'm going now," he said. "Don't wait up for me."

"I won't," she said. "But I'll worry."

He walked over and gave her a brotherly hug, broke it before anything else could happen.

"Good-bye, John," she said. "Take care."

"Good night, Laurie," he said and opened the door. Before she could call him back, he slipped around the house and walked slowly along the shadowed butte toward Deadfall.

He looked up at the sky and saw that there was no moon. It had yet to rise, he thought.

Perfect.

He thought of the town, what he had seen of it, and laid out his plan to slip past Main Street and start his patrol on a back street.

His senses tingled as if electrified.

He did not know what or who he would encounter.

But he loosened his pistol in its holster and walked slowly, stopped often to listen and look.

Until finally, he saw the town loom up in the darkness.

He stopped and let his eyes adjust to the absence of light.

He listened for any sound from man or beast.

He listened until he heard the muffled sound of a man clearing his throat.

It was enough for him to know that at least one man was on guard at the end of Main Street, hidden from view, cloaked in shadow, and waiting.

Just waiting.

18

Slocum flattened himself against the wall of the butte that bordered one side of the town.

A few yards away, he knew, stood a man on guard.

Slocum could hear him breathing in the stillness of the evening.

He scanned both sides of the street. In the distance he saw the glow of lamps in the windows of the boarding-house, saloon, and hotel. The rest of the street was pitch dark.

The man close to Slocum shuffled his boots. There was a crunch of boot on sand as the man shifted the position of his feet.

Slocum held his breath.

He could not see the man, but he knew he was very close.

Then, from the other side of the street, a voice called out in a loud whisper.

"Boze, you see anything yet?"

The man nearest to Slocum answered.

"No, Hack. Keep quiet."

So now Slocum knew the names of the men on watch at the end of Main Street.

The man closest to him was called Boze.

Slocum inched closer to where Boze stood. He was careful to set his boots down soft and not make any noise.

Closer still and Slocum froze.

Now he saw the man's head and the silhouette of his hat.

He slowed his own breathing. He estimated that he was no more than four or five feet away from Boze.

Boze turned his head.

Slocum's heart seemed to stop beating. His hand inched down to the butt of his Colt .45. He gripped it with slow deliberate flexes of his fingers. He held the pistol butt in his soft grip.

Boze wasn't looking in Slocum's direction.

He was staring at the man called Hack and then his head turned again and he was looking up Main Street.

That's when Slocum slid away from the butte wall and drew his pistol.

He shoved the barrel into the small of Boze's back. Hard.

Then Slocum placed his mouth next to Boze's ear and whispered into it very softly.

"You yell out or make any sound, Boze, and I'll blow a hole through your guts big enough to fill a hog trough."

Boze stiffened, but said nothing.

"Now, I've got one question for you, Boze," Slocum breathed. "Do you want to live or die? Just nod or shake your head. Nod for yes. Shake for no. Real slow."

Boze nodded that he wanted to live.

Slocum slid his hand down to Boze's pistol and lifted it out of its holster.

He tucked the pistol into his waistband.

"Now, you step out. Walk natural toward that other man, the one you called Hack. Don't say anything unless he calls out to you and then be very careful what you say."

Boze opened his mouth as if to reply, but said nothing.

Slocum pushed hard on his pistol. Boze stepped into the street. He headed for where Hack waited on guard. Slocum hung tight to Boze's back and matched him step for step.

Hack called out in a loud whisper, "Boze, what's up?"

"Don't answer him," Slocum said.

Boze walked on with Slocum right behind him like a Siamese twin.

"Something wrong, Boze?" Hack said, his voice rising in pitch.

Slocum jammed the barrel of his pistol hard into Boze's back.

"Say, 'Nope,'" Slocum whispered.

"Nope," Boze called out.

"You ain't supposed to leave your post, Boze."

When Boze was a few feet from Hack, Slocum jerked his pistol from Boze's back and smashed the butt of it into the back of the gunman's head.

Boze dropped like a sack of meal. He was knocked cold.

Hack took a step toward Boze, and Slocum closed the distance.

"What the hell?" Hack said.

"You make one move toward that hogleg, Hack, and you're a dead man."

Hack backed up a step. His hands came up to show that they were empty.

"Slocum?" he said as the tall man in black rammed the barrel of his pistol into Hack's gut.

"None other," Slocum said in a low voice.

"Jesus, don't shoot me," Hack said.

Slocum thumbed back the hammer so that Hack could hear the click.

Hack stiffened into a stone statue, his arms making a trident with his head in the middle.

"I'll give you the same choice as I gave Boze, Hack," Slocum said. "And I'm not Jesus."

"Yes, sir. Ask away."

"Do you want to live or die?"

Hack did not answer right away. His mouth opened but no sound came out.

Slocum pushed on the pistol. Hack's belly shrank two inches above his belt.

"Be quick, Hack," Slocum said. "This Colt has a hair trigger."

"Live," Hack blurted out. "I want to live."

"All right," Slocum said. He did not lessen the pressure of the barrel in Hack's midsection.

"Is—is Boze dead?" Hack asked.

"Not yet. His life and yours depend on what you say next. I want you to tell me where all the others who work for Canby are watching for me."

"I—I ain't sure."

"You've got three seconds," Slocum said. "My finger is starting to itch on the trigger."

"There's two others up at the start of Main Street. Them's all the ones I know about."

"Names?" Slocum said.

"Earl Cassaway and Roddie Nehring, I think."

"Those the two men I saw outside the hotel this morning?"

"I reckon. They said you was there with Obie and them gals."

"Where are those two gals?" Slocum asked.

"Uh, I think they're at the saloon. The Wild Horse."

"Where's Canby?"

"I don't know. Likely in the hotel, I reckon."

"Anybody staked out along Main Street?" Slocum asked.

Hack shook his head.

"Naw, I don't think so. Maybe some Mexes are lookin' around for you and Hornaday, but I don't know where they are."

"All right, Hack," Slocum said, "you and I are going to walk right up Main Street. Like we were friends or partners. You even twitch and you're dead meat."

"I'll do whatever you say, Slocum."

"That's Mr. Slocum to you, Hack."

"Yes, Mr. Slocum."

Slocum reached down and snatched Hack's pistol from his holster. He shoved it next to Boze's.

"Now we walk, Hack," Slocum said. "Real slow. When we get to where Cassaway and Nehring are, you call them out."

"Yes, sir, Mr. Slocum."

Slocum looked at Hack in disgust. He and Boze were both cut from the same bolt of cloth.

Both were cowards. Backshooters. They were brave enough when the odds were in their favor or they had the jump on a man, but when they faced the black hole of a Colt .45, their insides turned to jelly.

"Real slow, Hack. Like you were out for a stroll."

He shoved Hack toward Main Street. Hack walked slightly ahead of him.

Slocum rammed the barrel of his pistol into Hack's side.

Slocum looked on both sides of the street, waited for anyone to challenge them.

He hoped Boze would sleep a long time. He had hit him pretty hard and heard the crack of bone when the butt of his pistol struck Boze's skull.

They passed the boardinghouse then the saloon, with the lamps burning inside, the sounds of trumpets, guitars, and drums wafting onto the street. Through the windows, Slocum could see that it was crowded. He saw young glitter girls walking between tables carrying trays.

The hotel was quiet with lamps burning in the lobby and in some of the windows on the second and third floors. He saw no faces in the windows.

So far, he thought, so good.

The street was dark the rest of the way.

Stars peppered the black sky with glints of winking silver, but the moon was nowhere in sight.

"Just tell me where those two men are before we get there," Slocum told Hack in a low voice.

"Pretty close now, I think," Hack said.

"Just tell me where you think they are," Slocum said.

"There's a gatehouse off to the left," Hack whispered. "Ain't used no more, but—"

"Never mind the history," Slocum said. "Is one of the men in there?"

"Probably," Hack said.

"And the other man?"

"On the right is a little *tienda*. Roddie might be standin' somewhere around that store."

"We'll see," Slocum said. "When I say stop, you stop."

Hack nodded.

They walked to the end of the street.

"Hey, who the hell's out there?" a voice called from the deep shadows of the abandoned gatehouse.

"Tell him you're here," Slocum said.

"Cass, it's me, Hack."

"Stop," Slocum said. He eased the hammer of his pistol down to half cock, holding the trigger in slightly so that the mechanism would not make a sound.

Both men stopped.

"Who's that with you, Hack? Boze?"

"Tell him yes," Slocum said.

"Yeah," Hack said.

"What the hell you doin' way up here?" Cassaway yelled from the safety of the gatehouse.

"Tell him you caught me and Hornaday," Slocum said.

"We got 'em, Cass," Hack said. "We got Slocum and Hornaday."

"Sure enough. Hell, that's good news."

A man stepped away from the little store.

It was Roddie Nehring. He walked toward Slocum and Hackberry.

Cassaway emerged from the gatehouse and sauntered toward Slocum and Hack.

"Hell, I was about to shoot you, Hack," Nehring said.

Then he stopped.

"Hey," he yelled, "that ain't Boze. Who you got with you, Hack?"

Slocum stepped away from Hack.

"Both of you lighten your load," Slocum ordered. "Drop those pistols and come here."

"Shit," Roddie said.

He turned and started to run back to the store.

Slocum thumbed the hammer of his pistol to full cock.

"You won't make it, boy," Slocum said.

They all heard the click of the cocked hammer.

Nehring stopped.

"Drop your pistol quick, son, or you'll meet your maker," Slocum said.

Nehring just stood there, his back to Slocum and Hack.

Slocum caught sight of Cassaway out of the corner of his eye.

The man was inching his hand toward the pistol on his hip.

Time seemed to stand still and hover for those few

seconds. The music from the saloon died away and there was a silence along Main Street.

Slocum faced two armed men.

He waited, giving them both a chance to make up their minds.

Hack began to shake all over as if he were gripped with a sudden fever. Slocum could almost feel the tenseness in the man next to him.

He wondered if his pistol held the power of life or death as his finger curled around the trigger.

It was their move and Slocum was ready.

19

Slocum knew that Nehring would have to turn around to draw his pistol and open fire.

Cassaway was the most immediate threat.

"You touch that pistol, Cassaway, and you'll be stone dead before you clear leather," Slocum said in an even tone of voice.

Nehring wheeled to face Slocum. He went into a fighting crouch and slapped his hand on the butt of his pistol. His palm struck the leather of the holster and made a loud sound.

Slocum thought fast.

First, he shoved Hack face first to the ground and swung his pistol around to cover Roddie.

As Roddie drew his own pistol, Slocum quickly adjusted his vision to account for the distortion of night. He squeezed the trigger as Roddie brought up the barrel of his pistol.

Slocum's aim was true.

Roddie clutched his belly and staggered forward. His pistol slipped from his hand without being fired.

"You . . . you," he growled.

Then, Roddie crumpled up and collapsed.

Slocum swung his pistol to bear on Cassaway.

Again he had to allow for the vision shift in darkness.

Cassaway pulled his pistol halfway out of its holster.

On the ground, Hack groaned and spit dirt and grit from his mouth.

Slocum's pistol barked. Fire and lead streaked from the muzzle of his Colt .45.

The bullet caught Cassaway on his breastbone, shattering it. Splinters of bone shot through his heart and lungs.

Cassaway grunted, then pitched forward, his gun hand limp.

His pistol slid back into its holster as he fell, mortally wounded.

Slocum stepped over to Hack and came down hard on the small of his back with one heavy thump of his boot.

Cassaway spluttered, spewed blood onto the ground as the hole in his back gushed blood.

There was a stillness as the smoke from Slocum's gun hung like wispy cobwebs in the air.

The smell of burnt powder was strong and Slocum heard the echo of his last shot fade away somewhere down the street in Gravel Gulch.

Hack groaned under Slocum's boot.

"Are—are they both dead?" he asked.

"Nehring's gutshot," Slocum said.

He lifted his boot from Hack's back.

"You can get to your feet, Hack."

Hack pushed up from the ground and gathered his feet in a spraddle. He stood up, tottered for a moment, and then steadied as he regained his balance.

Nehring moaned from a few yards away.

Slocum prodded Hack with the barrel of his pistol and they both walked to where Roddie lay.

He looked up at them, but they could not see his eyes.

"Damn you, Slocum," Roddie swore.

"I'd say you were the one who is damned, Nehring."

Nehring sobbed as the pain shot through his belly and coursed up his spine.

"You—you won't get far, Slocum," Roddie said before he convulsed from the pain. He held a bloody hand to his belly, but Slocum could smell the stench of his intestines. They were bulging from his back like slithering snakes, oily and glistening in the dim light.

"He ain't got long," Hack said.

"He made his choice," Slocum said. "It was the wrong one."

"Go to hell, Slocum," Nehring gasped.

"I've been there several times, Nehring," Slocum said. "You're on your way."

Roddie twisted into a ball and struggled to breathe. His breath rattled in his throat as blood gushed up from his belly.

He spewed blood on the ground with his last expulsion of air.

He never drew another breath. He went into a final spasm and died, his mouth open like a beached fish.

"Christ," Hack breathed.

"Let's get out of here," Slocum said.

Patrons poured out of the Wild Horse Saloon down the street. Some stood there in the center of the street and looked both ways.

Slocum prodded Hack over to the dark buildings adjacent to the one where Nehring had stood guard. He pushed Hack against one of them and hugged the place next to him.

Then he opened his cylinder and pushed the rod through

the cylinders with the spent shells. They fell to the ground. He slid two fresh cartridges into the emptied cylinders, shoved the cylinder back in place, then shoved the barrel into Hack's side.

"You goin' to shoot me, Slocum?"

"Not yet, Hack," Slocum said. "We'll wait until it quiets down, then make our way back to where we left your pard, Boze."

"Some of the folks are walkin' this way," Hack said.

"Then we'll walk the other way," Slocum said.

He pushed Hack ahead of him to the gap between buildings and then toward the back, where they would not be seen.

Slocum took his time.

At each gap between stores, he stopped and they both saw people milling around.

They heard voices and then a shout as someone discovered the bodies of Cassaway and Nehring.

Slocum heard Mexican voices conversing in Spanish.

"You recognize any of those Mexicans, Hack?" Slocum asked.

"Yeah, a couple. I don't understand what they're sayin', though."

"They work for Canby?"

"Yep. One of 'em's named Rodrigo, the other'n I think is Paco."

The voices faded, but Slocum knew those two Mexicans were looking for him.

One of them mentioned the name *Salazar* and said they had to find him. The other spoke of someone named Ruben. He heard one man say the name *Machado*.

"Who is Ruben?" Slocum whispered to Hack.

"Ruben Machado. He works for Canby. Look, Slocum, all them Mexes are dead-aim shooters. If they catch up to you, it won't be like Cassaway and Nehring. Them Mexes grew up on bullets."

"I want to show you something when we can get some light, Hack."

"We ain't goin' to get no light behind these buildings," Hack said.

They walked farther behind the log stores until they were opposite the saloon.

There, between two stores, there was a faint finger of light.

Slocum pushed Hack alongside one store until they were just on the edge of the street.

There, the lamps from the saloon beamed enough light so that he could show Hack what he wanted him to see.

Slocum pulled the flyer from his pocket. He unfolded it. Then he held it in front of Hack.

"Can you read, Hack?" he asked.

"I had schoolin'. Yeah, I can read."

"Read this, then," Slocum said.

Hack was slow, but he read every word. He looked at the drawing a long time before Slocum snatched the paper away, folded it up, and put it back in his shirt pocket.

"Recognize anybody?" Slocum asked.

"That drawing looks a lot like Orson."

"And there's a bounty on his head."

"Yeah, there is. Is Canby—"

"Yep, his real name is Collins."

"You been huntin' him?"

"A long time," Slocum said.

"You ain't never goin' to catch him, Slocum. Canby's too damned smart."

"Maybe. We'll see. Come on. Let's see how Boze is doing."

Slocum and Hack walked behind the rest of the buildings to the end of Main Street, where it bled into the valley.

Boze was no longer there.

"He—he's gone," Hack said.

"Sure looks like it, Hack. Now the question is, what should I do with you?"

Hack turned and tried to see Slocum's face. Tried to look into his eyes.

Slocum's eyes were two black holes. His face was a mask.

"I—I don't know," Hack said. "Maybe let me go?"

"I could make you promise to ride out of Deadfall and not look back," Slocum said.

"You could."

"Trouble is, could I count on you to keep that promise?"

"I reckon you could. I've had my fill of Canby."

"Yeah, maybe," Slocum said softly.

"You got my gun, Slocum. If you killed me, you'd be the same as Orson, a murderer."

"That's so," Slocum said.

He did not want to kill Hack. At this point, it would be tantamount to murder.

By now, Boze was probably spilling his guts to Canby.

Canby would have men combing the town and valley for both him and Hornaday. Especially for him.

Now that Hack knew the truth about Canby, maybe he wanted no more of a man with a price on his head. Or he might be loyal to Canby, no matter what.

Slocum weighed his choices as he stood there with Hack.

The choices were few.

"Where's your horse and saddle, Hack?" Slocum asked.

The voices down the street began to die away, become more muffled and infrequent.

"I got a place in town," Hack said. "A cabin with a lean-to shelter and small corral out back. It's on the same street as the jail."

"If we cross the street, somebody might see us," Slocum said.

"They might."

"Worth a try, though."

"You goin' to let me go?" Hack asked.

"I'm thinking about it. I could take you to your place, watch you saddle up, and ride off. But how far would you go before you turned back and started to hunt me again?"

"If I rode out of here, I wouldn't come back," Hack said.

"That's what you say."

"That's what I mean, Slocum."

Hack was a hired gun as far as Slocum knew. Nothing more, nothing less.

But, he wondered, was Hack a man of his word?

"Let's put it this way, Hack," Slocum said. "I'll let you ride out. You take grub enough to get you somewhere else. That fair enough?"

"More than fair," Hack said.

"But I have a promise to you, Hack."

"What's that?"

"If I ever see you in Deadfall again, I won't ask questions. I'll just shoot you dead. On the spot."

Hack gulped empty air.

"You won't never see me in Deadfall again if you let me go, Slocum."

"I'll even give you your pistol back once I unload it," Slocum said.

"That's right generous of you, Slocum. That pistol is my stock-in-trade."

"Take my advice and take up another profession— shopkeeper, stage driver, or box loader."

Hack did not reply.

They walked to the edge of the street. Slocum looked both ways. There were no more people in front of the saloon, the boardinghouse, or the hotel. There were men carrying the bodies of Cassaway and Nehring toward a building beyond the hotel.

Nobody seemed to be looking toward the end of Main Street.

"Let's go, Hack," Slocum said quietly. "Walk fast, but don't run, to the next street."

The two men walked briskly across the street and vanished into the darkness without being challenged.

It was a long shot, Slocum thought, but maybe Hack would be true to his promise.

Besides, he had more to do that night, and he couldn't carry extra baggage.

What he had to do next, he had to do alone.

And it was, by far, more dangerous than anything he had been through that night.

20

Walt Bozeman was in the hot seat.

And he had a headache.

Orson Canby was hopping mad and for good reason.

"I gave you and Hack specific orders," Orson said.

"Hack was supposed to be on one corner at the end of Main Street and Rodrigo on the other."

"I know," Boze said. "I couldn't find Rodrigo."

"You were supposed to patrol Main Street. Instead, you got whacked on the head. Hack is gone and now Cassaway and Nehring are dead. A hell of a mess."

"I was fixin' to find Rodrigo and set him where I was standin'," Boze said. "I just kind of waited too long where I was."

"Kind of? You waited too damned long."

"I couldn't find Rodrigo, Orson. But I figured he would come along, so I stayed put."

"And now you got a headache," Orson said.

"Hurts like fire, boss."

"I don't give a damn," Orson said.

"Anyways, Slocum come out of nowhere, Orson. Crept up behind me and stuck a pistol in my back."

"So he didn't come from town," Orson said. It was not a question.

"Nope. He sure had to come out of that valley, out of Gravel Gulch."

"That's what I'm thinking," Orson said. "So he was holed up with one of those prospectors maybe."

"Or maybe camped out in one of the mines."

"Which one, I wonder," Orson said.

"Take you, us, maybe two whole days to search along those buttes, Orson."

Orson sat back in his easy chair. He had a bottle of whiskey and a half-filled tumbler on the little table next to him. There was a humidor filled with his cigars next to the whiskey glass and a box of lucifers within easy reach.

He had heard the gunshots, like most everybody else in town, and had wondered what was going on at the upper end of Main Street. He found out when Rodrigo came up and told him that Cassaway and Nehring had been shot dead at the upper end of Main.

"You were supposed to be standing guard at the entrance of the valley, Rodrigo," Orson had said.

"I got mixed up," Rodrigo told him. "I thought I was supposed to meet Boze at the Wild Horse. He never came."

"So you were in the saloon?"

"I was not drinking. I was waiting."

Orson had sent Rodrigo to look for Hack and Slocum, but he had returned with Boze, who had a nasty cut on the back of his head and was half-addled.

"Well, I sent Rodrigo down to where you and Hack were and told him to stay there all night if necessary. If he hears Slocum or Hack, he's supposed to open fire."

"On both of them?" Boze asked.

"Yeah, on both of them. Hack was as stupid as you, Boze. He let himself be taken prisoner by Slocum."

"Slocum's as sneaky as they come," Boze said.

"That he is. That's what makes him a menace. A dangerous man."

"He's probably killed Hack, too," Boze said.

Orson opened the humidor and extracted a cigar. He examined it a foot from his eyes, then reached in his pocket and brought out a sliding trimmer. He held the device and cigar over the ashtray. He inserted the cigar partways through the hole, pulled back on the tube, then pushed it back until it seated. The tip of the cigar fell into the ashtray. He put the cigar in his mouth, picked up the matchbox, opened it, and pulled out a match. He struck the matchhead against the sandpaper side of the box and held the flame to the cigar.

Boze watched him as if hypnotized.

Orson drew smoke into his mouth and throat, then expelled a cloud a few inches from his mouth.

"Slocum could be hiding almost in plain sight, Boze," Orson said.

"Huh?"

"You go on over to Hack's place and take a look. Slocum might be inside Hack's cabin."

Boze's eyes widened.

"Yeah, he could be there at that," Boze said.

"On the way to Hack's, you stop in at Ruben Machado's. Tell him this, will you?"

"What?" Boze asked.

"Tell Ruben to get Salazar and take that wagon full of rifles out tonight."

"Take it where?" Boze asked.

Orson smiled with the cigar in the center of his mouth.

"He knows where. You just be sure and tell him to haul ass right away. Got that?"

"Yeah, sure, boss. I'll tell him and then I'll scout Hack's place and see if maybe him and Slocum are there."

"Then report back to me," Orson said. "Be quick about it."

Boze stood up. "Slocum took my pistol, Orson. I don't have no way to defend myself."

"There's three drawers in that gun cabinet yonder, Boze. Second drawer down, you'll find some pistols. They're loaded. Take one and get the hell out of here and find Slocum."

"Yes, sir," Boze said.

He walked to the gun cabinet, opened the middle drawer, and pulled out a Colt .45 with stag grips. He hefted it and then slid it into his holster.

"This'll do fine," he told Orson, then turned toward the door.

He slouched out of the room and closed the door behind him.

Orson stood up and walked to the window. He looked down at the dark stretch of Main Street with its flickering shadows from the hotel lobby lamps and the Wild Horse Saloon.

There wasn't a sign of life.

"We ain't through with you yet, Slocum," he said to himself.

He puffed on the cigar and blew smoke against the windowpane. The smoke flattened out and spread across the glass like a soft thin glaze.

Then Orson walked to the gun cabinet and took out a loaded derringer pistol. It fit neatly into a long pocket on his vest. He tucked the pistol inside and patted it for reassurance.

"Just in case," he murmured to himself.

21

Slocum watched as Hack saddled up his horse and placed a sack of hardtack and beef jerky in one of the saddle-bags.

Moments later, he watched as Hack rode down Second Street and turned the corner, headed out of town.

He walked back behind the log huts and saw two Mexicans in a wagon at the back of the hotel.

One of the men stood in the bed, while the other sat on the seat, holding the reins for the two horses in his hands.

"*Andale*, Paco," the man in the driver's seat called out.

Paco lifted three or four carbines and restacked them in the wagon bed. He cursed in Spanish and then lifted more rifles and placed them with the others.

Slocum figured the wagon was full of rifles, and he saw what looked like ammunition boxes stacked near the front of the bed.

"These guns are all loose back here," Paco said in Spanish, which Slocum understood.

"Hurry up," the driver said.

"Ruben, you son of bad milk," Paco said, "you could help. These rifles will break if I do not stack them tight."

Slocum now knew the names of the two Mexicans. But why so many rifles? Where were they taking them? And so much ammunition, too.

He had a good idea as Paco finished snugging down the carbines and climbed onto the buckboard seat.

He watched the wagon rumble off and turn toward Main Street.

One thing was for sure—those rifles were not going into the valley, but into the Arizona desert.

He thought of the smoke signals.

His stomach sank.

Those rifles and ammunition boxes could be going to only one place.

Somewhere, among the buttes and mesas of the desert, the Apaches were gathering. They were going to get Spencer repeating carbines, courtesy of one Orson Canby.

The thought made Slocum wince.

There could be only one reason why Canby would supply the Apaches with arms and ammunition.

He wanted them to raid the valley and slaughter all the miners and prospectors.

Then he would have the town to himself and could lay claim to all the mines.

Diabolical, Slocum thought.

Then, as the sound of the wagon faded away, Slocum had another thought.

Canby would have to give a signal to the raiding Apaches and then get the hell out of town.

That was the only way he could escape the carnage.

A plan began to form in Slocum's mind. There was a way to beat Canby and fend off the Apaches. He was sure of it.

For now, he had time to think it all through and prepare for what was bound to happen in Deadfall.

He stepped across the street and saw the back doors of the Wild Horse Saloon. There was a loading dock with steps on both sides.

He could hear the Mexican band playing a lively tune.

He climbed the steps and stood by the back doors for a few minutes.

Then he pulled on the handle of one door.

It opened.

Slocum slipped inside the back room like a shadow and waited.

He saw a young man silhouetted against the lamplight streaming down the hallway from the main hall. Then the man disappeared and the way was clear.

Slocum walked to the entrance to the dance hall and stepped out.

He saw an empty table nearby and sat down at it, squinting as his eyes adjusted to the light.

He looked around.

Nobody had noticed him.

Then he saw Renata gliding between tables where men were seated with mugs of beer in front of them. More movement caught his eye and he turned his head slowly and removed his hat.

He placed his hat on the chair next to him.

Now, he thought, he might not be so conspicuous.

A young Mexican dressed in a skimpy glitter gal costume noticed him and walked over, a tray in her hands.

"Sir, I did not see you. May I serve you something?"

"Bring me a beer," Slocum said.

She smiled and curtsied, then turned around.

In another part of the saloon, Slocum caught sight of

Bonnie. She was walking toward him with an empty tray, but she pretended not to notice him.

Moments later, Bonnie stood in front of him.

"John," she whispered, "what are you doing here? Don't you know that Canby's men are looking all over for you?"

"I just wanted to see how you and Renata are doing," he said quietly.

"We—we feel like prisoners. Marlene, that woman sitting over there with a bunch of men, makes us take these smelly men up to our rooms and—"

"I get the idea," Slocum said. "You're unhappy, then."

"Yes. Very," she said.

Slocum looked over at the table where Marlene sat surrounded by garrulous men.

"I have to go, John," Bonnie said. "You'd better go, too, before Canby's men find you."

Bonnie walked away and headed for the bar.

The Mexican girl came back with a glass of beer on a tray.

"One dime," she said.

Slocum gave her a two-bit piece. She thanked him, then walked away with her empty tray.

Across the room, the woman he took to be Marlene looked over at him.

Slocum lifted the mug to his lips and drank. Then he hoisted the glass a few inches and looked at Marlene.

He smiled.

Marlene smiled back, then arose from the table. He saw her lean down and bid the men farewell.

She headed straight for his table, slinky and curvaceous in her black satin gown with its low-cut bodice. Her earrings dangled and sparkled with light from the saloon lamps.

The band played on as Marlene approached Slocum at his table.

22

Marlene Vanders did not miss much. As the manager of the Wild Horse Saloon, very little escaped her scrutiny.

When she saw the man dressed in black talking to Bonnie, her interest perked considerably. And the more she stared at the stranger, the more fascinated she became.

He did not resemble any of the miners or prospectors who frequented her watering hole, and he certainly was a cut or two above the gunmen Canby had on his payroll.

No, there was something decidedly different and distinctive about the man she saw at the table near the back entrance. And when he took off his hat, her gaze took in his thick black hair, the way it flowed down the back of his neck above his broad shoulders.

He looked and acted like a courtly Southern gentleman, and she knew he didn't belong in Deadfall, any more than she did.

She walked over to the tall man's table after Bonnie had left. Leaning close to him, she asked, "May I join you?"

"By all means, ma'am," Slocum said. He stood up and

pulled out a chair for her. She sat down and he scooted the chair closer to the table before he sat back down.

"I'm Marlene Vanders," she said. "I own this establishment. May I ask your name, sir?"

"My name is Jack Smith," Slocum lied.

"Sure it is," she said with a merry twinkle in her eye. "And I'm Little Bo Peep."

Slocum laughed.

"Buy you a drink?" he said.

"Why, I would be flattered," she said. "But I only partake of soda water when I'm working."

"You look mighty elegant for a working gal," he said.

Marlene smiled. Her smile was warm and friendly.

"You know you're taking a chance coming in here, don't you, Mr. Slocum?"

"Call me John," he said.

"I thought it was Jack," she retorted.

"I answer to many names, ma'am."

Slocum sipped his drink. Marlene raised her hand. In a few moments, one of the Mexican glitter girls appeared at the table carrying a tray with a glass of soda water on it.

"Thank you, Teresa," she said. "Mr. Smith will pay you for my drink."

"That will be one bit," Teresa said.

Slocum reached into his pocket and laid a quarter on the tray.

Teresa curtsied, then left to go back to the bar. That was after she batted her long black lashes and winked at Slocum.

"I came here to check on the two new gals you hired today, Miss Vanders," Slocum said.

"Please, John. Call me Marlene."

"Yes'm."

"You mean Bonnie and Renata, I assume. Why, they're

doing just fine. As if they were born to the task of serving my patrons."

"I hope you pay them what they're worth," Slocum said.

Marlene took a sip of her drink and cocked her head.

"Do I detect a faint drawl in your speech, John? You're not from Arizona Territory, by no means, are you?"

"Georgia, ma'am, Calhoun County. Born and raised."

"I thought so. I'm originally from Mississippi myself, and I must tell you I miss the Southern charm of the folks down South."

Slocum sipped his beer.

He looked at Marlene and she was beautiful. But his gaze roamed over the room, and in a far corner, he spotted Obie Gump, who had not seen him. He hoped the wagon driver would not look his way and walk over. It would be awkward and could turn ugly in a hurry if he were to bandy the name of Slocum about.

"John, I had a talk with Bonnie and Renata about their trip out here as would-be brides. They had some interesting things to say about you."

"I'm sure," Slocum said.

Marlene smiled.

"They said that not only did you save their lives from the Apaches, but that you proved to be an ingenious and innovative lover."

"Nice girls don't tell," Slocum said as he glanced over her head at new men at the batwing doors. Men he did not know.

"They were anxious to share their experiences with you," Marlene said. "Did you find them to be pleasurable?"

"Men don't discuss women in saloons. Especially with such a beautiful woman as you, Marlene."

"You flatter me, John."

"You are a beautiful woman," Slocum said.

"A desirable one?"

"Very," he said.

She threaded her hair with delicate fingers and tossed her head back like a proud woman.

"I find you very attractive. Handsome in a certain way," she said.

"You flatter me, as well," he said.

"Men usually do not interest me," she said. "But there is something about you that draws me to you. Maybe it's your toughness combined with a gentility that is a trait of some Southern men, or maybe it's that you exude a masculinity that is, well, almost primitive. Like a wild wolf that has been partly tamed."

She smiled again, almost as if she had surprised herself.

Slocum did not say anything just then. He was still trying to figure her out, he admitted. She was as mysterious as she was beautiful. But so far, he felt no stirring of desire. There was something cold about Marlene, something lovely that was made of iron.

The men walked into the saloon, but did not look around the room. Instead, they headed for the nearest table. They looked like hard-rock miners with their chambray shirts, flannel trousers, and heavy work boots. They wore no sidearms.

Marlene sipped her soda water.

Slocum hoisted his beer and drained the glass.

"So you want another?" she asked.

"No, this is a one-beer night for me, I reckon," he said.

"Why? Are you going somewhere?"

"I am," he said. "Soon."

"Where?"

"Curiosity killed the cat," he said.

"My, you're certainly fond of quaint homilies, John. I almost get the feeling that you don't really want to talk to me."

"I did not mean to give you that impression," he said.

"You know, my quarters are right behind this wall," she said. "Just beyond the stairwell."

"Are you inviting me to your room?"

She leaned forward.

"I'm thinking that if we were alone in a more gracious atmosphere, I might find out more about you."

"What you see, Marlene, is pretty much what you get with me."

"I doubt that," she said.

At that moment, the batwing doors swung open and a man bulled his way into the saloon.

He was glaring in challenge to any man in his path, but he was looking straight at Slocum.

Slocum reached over to the other chair and picked up his hat. He put it on and sat there for a moment, ready to spring to his feet.

"Are you leaving so soon, John?" Marlene asked.

"It looks like I might have to," he said.

He looked beyond her with his green eyes fixed on something. She turned around to see what he was looking at with such intensity.

There, in clear view, stood a man she knew.

He began to walk directly toward their table.

He looked ready to fight.

Slocum's right hand slid down his trousers to land on the butt of his pistol.

Marlene gasped.

The man approaching them was Walt Bozeman. The one they called Boze.

Men cleared a path for Boze.

Then they all looked toward the table where Marlene sat with Slocum.

Slocum braced himself for a gunfight he did not want.

23

Boze drew his pistol and yelled for all to hear.

"I saw you in the winder, Slocum. Now I'm gunnin' for you."

Boze started to shoot. He fired one shot, then another.

Slocum, instead of drawing his own pistol, took the shortest distance between two points.

He reached for Boze's other gun in his waistband and pulled it out. He thumbed back the hammer to full cock, pushed the table over, and raised the pistol to take aim.

Boze charged straight toward Slocum. He fired wildly.

Bullets ricocheted off the wall and ripped through the table.

Slocum shoved Marlene to one side with such force that she fell to the floor.

Bonnie, Renata, and the two Mexican gals all screamed at different pitches.

Slocum took aim and squeezed the trigger of Boze's pistol.

He misjudged and the shot went astray. The bullet

whistled past Boze's ear and thunked into one of the batwing doors. Splinters sprayed from the door in several different directions.

Boze fired off all six shots in the cylinder of his revolver.

The last shot sizzled past Slocum's ear.

Still, Boze charged on, his eyes blazing with hatred and determination.

Slocum held the gun at arm's length. Boze's chest grew large beyond the blade front sight. Slocum squeezed the trigger. The pull was stronger than his own hair trigger, but the muzzle erupted with flame and sparks.

Boze staggered as the bullet smashed into his chest, just below the breastbone.

He stopped and regained his footing. Then he opened the cylinder and slid it to the side of the pistol. He pushed the ramrod and one of the hulls fell to the floor. Spinning the cylinder, he pumped the ramrod to eject the other empty cartridges.

Then he began to pull cartridges from his gun belt and stuff them into the empty chambers.

Blood spurted from his midsection and dribbled down to his crotch.

Slocum waited until Boze looked up at him after slamming the cylinder back into place.

Everyone in the saloon heard the snick of the hammer as Boze thumbed it back to full cock.

Slocum stepped around the overturned table and took deadly aim. He squeezed the trigger when the blade front sight lined up with the rear buckhorn on the center of Boze's forehead.

The pistol bucked in his hand as it exploded with burning powder that pushed the bullet at high speed through the barrel and out the muzzle.

The lead slug smashed into Boze's skull, leaving a black hole dead center.

The back of Boze's head blew apart. Bone and brain matter flew backward and to both sides. The mush spattered some of the nearby patrons and one of the bartenders. They all ducked, but the damage was done.

Boze crumpled and his hand loosened. His pistol dropped from limp fingers. He collapsed in a heap as blood spewed from his forehead and puddled up in the cavern at the back of his skull.

Slocum walked over to the dead man and dropped the pistol just in front of Boze's head. It hit the floor with a metallic thud.

"Here's your pistol back, Boze," Slocum said.

Then he touched a finger to his hat and walked through the batwing doors.

There was a silence in the saloon.

Wisps of gun smoke hung in the air over the dead man. There was the acrid smell of burnt powder around the body and by the table Slocum had kicked over with his boot.

Nobody moved for several seconds. Then pandemonium set in as the room erupted with gabble.

Obadiah walked over and stood next to Boze. He looked at the clamoring crowd. The glitter girls were still stooped over in fright and shock.

Marlene rose to her feet.

"That was Slocum," Obie announced. "And he shot Boze with his own pistol."

Men cried out in surprise and the room filled with their astonished clamor.

Obie held up his hands for quiet.

"Now Slocum is a hunted man. But as you just saw, he don't go down easy. I seen his pistol work before, and I'm tellin' all of you, he ain't a man to back down to nobody."

The saloon erupted in cheers from the miners and prospectors. They began to raise their glasses and shout out toasts to the man in black.

Bonnie stood up straight and looked over at Renata.

They exchanged meaningful looks.

Marlene spoke to one of the bartenders.

"Cletus," she said, "clean up that mess on the floor."

Then she walked back to where the musicians were still cowering next to the bandstand.

"Play some lively music," she said to the bandleader. *"Toca, toca."*

Slowly, each man in the small orchestra climbed back on the stage. When they were settled, they began to play spirited Spanish music, the kind heard at bullfights. And gradually, the saloon quieted down as men exchanged views of what they had seen and heard.

Slocum hugged the buildings on the far side of Main Street.

He walked with slowness and deliberateness, his senses alert for any sound or sight.

He reached the end of the street and vanished into the starlit valley.

He headed for Laurie's, a weariness in him that was beyond any day laborer's fatigue. He was bushed and wanted only to kick off his boots and let the tiredness leak out of his bones.

And, too, there was Laurie, waiting for him on a beautiful evening.

24

Lamplight glowed in the front room of Laurie's cabin.

It was quiet when Slocum walked up and looked through the windows and saw her through the golden panes.

She was curled up on the divan, her bare legs showing beneath the flimsy wrap she wore over her pink nightgown. Her hair was glossy with a dark sheen from the glow of the lamp.

He tapped softly on her door.

Laurie opened it and her face brightened when she saw Slocum standing there, light glancing off his dark coat and trousers.

"Oh, thank God, John," she exclaimed. "I was so worried about you. Come in. Please come in."

He walked through the door and Laurie closed it behind him. She dropped the latch.

"Here," she said, "sit on the divan. Tell me all about what happened tonight."

He sat down and she curled up next to him. He took off his hat and set it on the floor.

"In my saddlebags," he said, "back in the room you gave me, you'll find a bottle of Kentucky bourbon. I'd be obliged if you would fetch it for me so we can both have a drink."

"Oh yes," she cooed and rose from the couch. She dashed out of the room and he heard a door open. A few moments later, she was there with the bottle of whiskey. She set it on the small table in front of the couch and then raced to the kitchen. He heard cupboard doors squeak as she opened them. Then, the clink of glasses. She came back into the room with two empty tumblers with thick glass bottoms. She set them on the table.

"Shall I pour?" she asked.

"By all means," he said, and ran his fingers through his thick black hair.

Laurie poured two fingers of whiskey in each tumbler. She handed one of the glasses to Slocum. She held her glass up to her mouth and sniffed the whiskey.

"It smells good," she said.

"It tastes even better," he said as he upended his glass and drank a small amount. The whiskey warmed his throat as it went down and he felt its heat in his stomach. His shoulders dropped the weight he had been carrying as if by magic.

"John, please tell me what you did tonight. Did anyone try to capture or kill you?"

Slocum told her all that had transpired after he left her. He did not mention the glitter girls or Marlene.

"It's those guns I'm worried about. Sure as I'm sitting here, Canby has sent them to the Apaches. Those smoke signals told me part of the story. I don't know the rest."

"What do you think the Apaches will do with those rifles?" she asked.

Slocum took another sip of the smooth whiskey.

"My guess is that Canby has an alliance with the Apaches. I shot one of the Mexicans who was dressed like an Apache. That shows me that there is a definite connection. The Mexican worked for Canby, according to Obie, the wagon driver."

"So what will the Apaches do?" she asked. She had yet to taste the whiskey, but she held up her glass in readiness.

"I think Canby wants it all," Slocum said. "If he has the Apaches kill all the miners and prospectors, he can file claims on everything in this valley and probably wind up a very rich man."

"Oh, John, that's so outrageous. Why, just the thought of him doing that makes my skin crawl."

"Mine, too," he said. "But that's what it looks like."

"What are you going to do?" she asked. "What are any of us going to do? If those Apaches attack us . . ."

"Tomorrow, I want to talk to all the good men of Deadfall," Slocum said. "I'll tell them what they must do if we are all going to survive."

"Yes," she said. "I'll help you. I know most everyone here who is honest and hardworking."

"I'll need your help, Laurie."

She sipped the whiskey and felt its fire slide down her throat. She gasped for air and set her glass down.

"When you were in the Wild Horse, did you happen to see the owner, Marlene Vanders?" Laurie asked.

"I saw her," Slocum said.

"Did you talk to her?"

Slocum wiped his lips.

"I talked to her," Slocum said, avoiding eye contact with Laurie.

She slid closer to him and took another sip of whiskey.

"She's a very beautiful woman, isn't she, John?" Laurie said, without a trace of venom in her voice.

But Slocum knew that this impression was deceptive. She was trying to find out what he thought of Marlene without asking him a direct question.

Feminine wiles, he thought.

"I didn't notice that much," Slocum said.

Laurie scooted closer to him.

She set down her glass.

Then she tucked a finger under his chin and turned his head so that he could look into her eyes.

"Funny thing about Marlene," she said. "So far as I know, she has not set her sights on any of the men in Deadfall. But I wouldn't be surprised if she was attracted to you, John."

Slocum swallowed a ball of air in his throat. His Adam's apple bobbed.

Laurie reached over and ran fingers through his thick black hair.

"No," she said, "I wouldn't be surprised at all. You are a very attractive man."

"Laurie . . ."

She put a finger over his lips to silence him.

"There's a lot to do tomorrow," she said, her voice soft and mesmerizing. "Both of us are bound to have a busy day. We should both get some sleep. Are you hungry?"

He shook his head.

"Tired?"

"Some," he said.

"I hate to think of you sleeping all by yourself in that dreary little room of Harvey's."

"It's all right," he gruffed, gravel in his throat.

Laurie moved very close to him until her breasts were touching his arm. She rubbed them back and forth across his biceps.

Slocum swallowed again, his throat as dry as his mouth. The taste of whiskey on his tongue had vanished.

Then she leaned over and grasped the back of his neck. She kissed him hard on the lips and he felt her hand tighten against his nape.

He set down his glass and took Laurie in his arms.

She held the kiss, and her tongue raked his with delicate swipes that sent his temperature up by a degree or two.

Then he wrapped his arms around her and held her close.

Her hand slid down his back and she embraced him in a loving hug.

"Oh my," she breathed as she broke off the kiss. "I—I've never had such feelings about a man before."

Slocum saw her look deep into his eyes and said nothing.

They kissed again, more passionately than before. She squirmed against him and then one hand slid down to his crotch. She felt the bulge in his pants and gently squeezed.

Slocum's senses shifted into a high range and he felt his cock swell against his trousers.

Laurie felt it, too, and squeezed his member, then began to stroke it through his pants.

"We—we'd better retire to my bedroom," she said. "I think you have something I want."

They kissed again, then Laurie slid off his lap.

"There's something I want, too, Laurie."

She took his hand. They left the room like two sleep-walkers and entered her bedroom. A lamp burned next to her bed.

"Hurry," she said.

She slid her gown off, then slipped out of her negligee as Slocum unbuckled his gun belt, and began to unbutton his shirt. He was pulling his trousers off on the edge of her bed when she walked in front of him and stood there, totally nude.

"Beautiful," he said. His voice carried on a husky breath.

She posed for him as he shucked off his boots and slid his pants down to hit the floor in a puddle of cloth.

Slocum's lap told her that he was in full readiness. She reached over and grabbed his cock, and slowly slid her hand up and down its length as he sat there, looking at that dark thatch between her legs, the long clean lines of her legs, the slight pooch of her tummy, and the provocatively wide hips that were all woman.

She turned down the coverlet and slid past him into bed.

Slocum joined her there and his hand went to her pussy. He rubbed the wiry hairs and felt the softness of her labia. She squirmed with pleasure under the caress of his hand.

He slid a finger into the portal of her sex as he came close to her and she jolted with a sudden short spasm.

They kissed and he continued to stroke his finger in and out of her honey pot until she was moving her hips up and down in a slow rhythm.

She spread her legs and Slocum's finger came out of her pussy as he straddled her with his body.

He looked down at her. Her eyes were glazed with lust, and she held up her arms so that he could collapse into her embrace.

"Yes, now, John," she said, and he dipped his loins downward.

She grasped his rock-hard organ and guided it to the soft lips of her cunt.

Slocum slid in with a gentle push.

Inside, she was warm and wet. They kissed and her hand dropped away as he buried his cock into the pudding of her pussy.

Laurie sighed. Deeply.

John increased his rhythm by slow degrees. Up and down, in and out, until her body was pliable and lithe.

Then she screamed softly and convulsed as an orgasm rippled through her loins and shook her entire body. Her legs flew up and wrapped around his back.

He plunged even deeper into her moist warm cavern, touching the tip of her womb and stroking her clitoris until it vibrated like a tuning fork, turning her muscles into jelly.

"Oh, oh!" she screamed in his ear, and she bucked up against him with one jolting orgasm after another.

He held himself at bay for as long as he could. She was ravenous and raging with lust, and he used most of his willpower to keep from exploding his seed inside her.

Then he could no longer hold back the tide. He plummeted deep within her and felt the surge of energy as his jism spurted from the tiny eye of his prick. She raked his back with her fingernails and sighed deeply as she climaxed once again.

He heard a noise and saw her arm move. Her hand reached out and turned down the wick in the lamp, plunging the room into darkness.

Only the glow from the rising moon filled the room as he rolled off her body and lay sated next to her.

They held hands and kissed again. This time it was the kiss of two experienced and satisfied lovers.

The moonlight limned their bodies with an ethereal glow as their desire waned, then flared into life again a few moments later.

And their loving was deeper and more satisfying the second time.

They were alone and the night was kindly with the moon's pale light glistening like alabaster dust on the windows.

25

Slocum arose early while Laurie was still fast asleep. He dressed quickly, strapped on his gun belt, and left her cabin before the sun was up.

He walked over to Harvey's unfinished log cabin and saw lamps burning. Smoke curled from the chimney and he could smell the aroma of strong coffee when he knocked on the front door.

Harvey opened the door. He was dressed except he had no shirt on over the top of his long johns.

"John," he said. "What brings you here at such an early hour?"

"Wanted to talk to you before you went to the mine," Slocum said.

"Sure. Come on in. I just made a fresh pot of coffee. My eye opener. Join me?"

Slocum went in and Harvey closed the door, waved Slocum to a crude wooden chair that had no padding as yet. The cabin smelled of fresh logs and fresh-cut lumber in cabinets and tables.

Harvey walked to his kitchen and came back with two tin cups. He picked up the coffeepot on the potbellied stove in the front room and poured the cups nearly full.

They drank coffee and rubbed their overnight beard stubble.

"So, you came here for a reason so early, John. What is it?"

"I want to warn you, Harve, and show you something."

Slocum pulled the wanted flyer from his pocket, unfolded it, and handed it to Harvey.

Harvey read it quickly and looked long and hard at the drawing of Junius Collins.

Then he handed the flyer back to Slocum, who refolded it and slipped it back in his shirt pocket.

"I'm not very surprised," Harvey said. "But surprised. That's Orson Canby, I'm sure."

"It is. He murdered a friend of mine in Dodge City when he was called Junius Collins."

"So you're going to try and collect the bounty?"

"For his widow, yes," Slocum said.

"Well, good luck. Canby is surrounded by guns and men who know how to use them."

"That's not why I came over, Harvey," Slocum said.

Harvey sipped his coffee. His eyebrows arched.

"No? Why, then?"

"If you saw those smoke signals yesterday, you know the Apaches are up to something."

"I've seen smoke signals before. Not here, but on the way out here."

"Last night, a wagonload of guns left Deadfall and headed out to the desert. Spencer repeaters. Carbines. And ammunition. I think Canby is in cahoots with the Apaches. On the way here in Obie's wagon, we were attacked by some Apache braves."

"Oh?"

"Except one of them was a Mexican named Sanchez. Obie told me he worked for Canby."

"Yes. Fidel Sanchez. He was one of Canby's strong arms. Gave me and some other miners a hard time a couple of months ago. You killed him?"

"Yes. He was wearing Apache clothes. And war paint."

"Hmmm. Curious."

"More than curious, Harvey. I think Canby wants the Apaches to wipe out the settlement here so he can lay claim to all the holdings in this valley."

Harvey let out a low whistle.

"So," Slocum said. "From now on, carry your rifle with you when you go to and from your mine. There will be some kind of signal, I'm sure, which will give Canby a chance to light a shuck before the shooting starts."

"I'd better warn all my friends here," Harvey said.

"Laurie and I plan to ride out this morning and convey this message to everyone. If we stick together, we can drive the Apaches out of here before they slaughter every man in Deadfall."

"All right. Good idea. I can't possibly see every man here while I'm on foot."

Slocum finished his coffee and rose up from his chair.

He and Harvey shook hands.

"What about Canby?" Harvey asked.

Slocum started for the door.

"I'm going after him," Slocum said. "Today."

"Good luck."

"Watch your topknot, Harvey."

Slocum left and walked back to Laurie's cabin.

The sun was still in another part of the world.

He had a lot to do and very little time to accomplish all that needed to be done.

But, he thought, he had made a start.

26

Laurie was up and dressed by the time Slocum returned and entered her cabin.

She held a small pistol and holster in her hand.

Slocum recognized the items.

"You left this on the floor in my bedroom," she said. "At least I assume it's yours."

Slocum laughed and grabbed the small revolver and its case.

"My belly gun," he said.

"Where did you go so early this morning?" she asked.

Slocum attached the gun inside his trousers behind his belt buckle and told her that he had been to see Harvey.

They ate a quick breakfast and walked to town, where they headed for the stables. The sun was up, but there were still shadows on Main Street.

Johnny was there, feeding all the horses, when they walked in on him.

"You goin' for a ride, Miss Laurie?" Johnny said. "With him?"

"John, maybe you'd better talk to Johnny before we go. Show him that flyer you have."

While Laurie led her horse out of the stall, Slocum took Johnny aside and pulled the flyer from his pocket.

"Do me a favor, will you, Johnny?" he said as he made sure they were both out of earshot of Laurie.

"I don't know, Mr. Slocum. Mr. Canby would have my hide if he knew you were here and I didn't tell him."

"Oh, you can tell him I was here, Johnny," Slocum said. "But first, I want you to take this flyer and give it to Marlene Vanders at the Wild Horse. Do you know where her room is?"

"Yes, sir, I sure do. Everybody does. But she's probably still asleep. Till noon maybe."

"Wake her up and tell her I wanted her to have this."

Slocum handed the paper to the stable boy.

"What is it?" Johnny asked.

"You can take a look at it if you want. But you better do it before you tell Canby I was here."

"Where you goin', Mr. Slocum?"

"I wish I could tell you, Johnny, but now is not the time. Trust me. I'll see you later today maybe, or sometime tomorrow."

Johnny took the paper and tucked it into a shirt pocket.

Slocum saddled Ferro. He and Laurie rode back to her cabin so that he could get his saddlebags, rifle, and canteens.

She packed food and they rode out into the valley. By then the sun had cleared the buttes, the creeks were shining, and the valley lit up like an oil painting.

"Did you give that wanted flyer to Johnny?" she asked as they rode toward the far end of the valley, to where Hornaday was hiding out.

"Yes."

"Don't you think it would help to show that to all the men we're going to warn?"

"I have another one," Slocum said, and patted a pocket of his shirt.

"You're smarter than you look," she said, and smiled.

"Maybe I look smarter than I am," he said.

The sun was at their backs as they rode down the center of the valley. Men were already at the creeks with their pans and sluices, and men entered holes in the buttes that they had blasted and carved with pickaxes. They all waved as the two passed by.

"They won't be smiling when they hear what you have to say, John."

"And they'll have to empty out this valley and fetch their rifles and sidearms," he said. "There's probably not too many moments to lose."

"What will you tell them?" she asked as they headed for the mesa where Hornaday had spent the night in a cave.

"I'm going to tell them to prepare for war," he said.

"War?"

"War with the Apaches. I've got my own war to wage."

"Whatever are you talking about, John? Aren't you going to fight alongside the rest of us?"

"If I get the chance," he said. "But I've got a war of my own to fight."

She looked at him long and hard.

"Canby," he said. "Before he leaves town."

27

Shortly after noon, the empty wagon rolled up to a stop behind Mrs. Hobbs's boardinghouse. Rodrigo set the brake. He and Paco climbed down and entered the house through the back entrance.

Moments later, they carried out mattresses, pillows, and worn-out sheets and piled these in the bed of the wagon.

Then the two walked up to the hotel and went through the back doors.

They found Canby in Matt Jennings's office on the mezzanine. Both men stood near the open safe. They were placing stacks of money into saddlebags on Jennings's desk.

The Mexicans had never seen so much money before. And there were bags full of gold dust on the desk as well.

"Back already?" Canby said.

"Blue Wolf is coming," Rodrigo said. "When he sees the smoke, he will attack. Paco and I have the wagon loaded with the old mattresses and pillows like you said to get from Mrs. Hobbs. We are going to go to Gravel Gulch and leave it."

"We will soak the bedding with coal oil," Paco said. "Like you said, Orson."

"So, by late afternoon . . ." Canby said, exchanging looks with Jennings.

"That's fast, Orson," Jennings said.

"We'll be lucky to leave before they come."

Then he looked at Paco.

"When you boys leave, stop by the stables and tell Johnny to hitch those new horses to that covered wagon parked out back."

"I will do that," Paco said.

"After you boys light up that wagon, you better light out of town."

"Where do you go, Orson?" Rodrigo asked. "With all that money and gold?"

Canby smiled.

"West," he said. "Until the scalps are dry in the Apache lodges."

Both men backed out of the office and ran down the stairs.

They knew Blue Wolf would come, and they wanted to set fire to the wagon and light out themselves.

"We must take our saddles with us and ride those horses that pull the wagon," Rodrigo said.

"Yes. We must do that," Paco said.

They headed for the stables, driving the wagon full of worn-out bedding.

Their eyes were still wide from seeing all that money and gold.

28

Slocum rode back into Deadfall alone.

He had warned all the men in the valley and they had left town themselves as he had advised.

Laurie had gone back to her cabin.

Hornaday was with her. They both saw the wagon rumble into the valley.

They watched with binoculars as two Mexicans unhitched horses, saddled them, and then poured something over whatever was in the wagon bed.

Then both men struck matches and tossed them into the wagon.

The wagon erupted in a blaze of fire that turned to smoke.

The smoke rose straight up in the sky as if through an invisible chimney.

"Wallace," Laurie exclaimed. "That's the signal for the Apaches to attack. It's got to be."

"All hell's goin' to break loose pretty soon," he said as he gripped his rifle and looked at the column of smoke.

The two men climbed up on the saddled horses and rode off toward town at a gallop.

Slocum rode Ferro past the stables and headed for the hotel.

The sun had passed its zenith and was falling toward the west in a slow burning arc.

Just before he turned the corner of Second Street, he saw Johnny run toward him from the stables.

"Mr. Slocum, Mr. Slocum!" he called.

Slocum reined in Ferro and came to a halt.

"I gave that flyer to Miss Marlene," he said. "Like you told me to."

"Good, Johnny. Now you better get yourself a rifle and strap on a pistol."

"How come?"

Slocum looked back toward the valley and pointed.

"That's the signal to the Apaches," he said. "They're going to come through town like shit through a tin horn pretty quick."

"I looked at that flyer, Mr. Slocum. That's Canby, ain't it?"

"Afraid so, son."

"He had me hitch up them horses you sold him and he's loadin' up bags and suitcases and such right now. Like he's goin' on a long trip."

"Thanks, Johnny. Marlene say anything?" he asked.

"She said to thank you, Mr. Slocum. And . . . and she said she hoped she would see you again sometime."

"Better tell her about the Apaches, Johnny."

Slocum rode around the corner. Down the street, he saw Canby and a man he did not know, lifting bundles and satchels into a covered wagon. The four horses he had brought to Deadfall were hitched up and stomping their hooves.

He caught Canby by surprise. The man with him went wide-eyed as well.

"Slocum," Canby said.

"Junius," Slocum said.

Jennings's face turned white.

Slocum dismounted and slapped Ferro on the rump. The horse trotted off but then stopped and stood several yards away.

"You want to go easy, Canby, or hard?" Slocum said as he stood there, feet apart, his arms loose at his sides.

"I ain't goin' with you, if that's what you mean, Slocum. Me and Jennings here have other plans."

"You called it, Canby," Slocum said.

Just then a man stepped out of the hotel. He looked at Slocum in surprise.

It was Hack.

He started for his pistol, his hand diving like a hawk toward the butt of his Colt.

Slocum drew his pistol, cocked it on the rise.

"You made your choice, Hack," Slocum said. "Now die." He fired one shot, and Hack fell to the street.

Slocum turned as Jennings opened his coat and his hand floundered to reach the pistol hung high on his belt.

He shot Jennings in the face before the man could draw his weapon.

Canby had a derringer in his hand. He cocked it as Slocum swung his pistol.

Canby fired one round, which missed Slocum by several inches.

It was the last thing Canby ever did.

Slocum squeezed the trigger and shot Canby right through the heart. The blood spurt did not last long as the organ stopped pumping.

Canby collapsed into a pile of tailored cloth and blood.

Smoke lazed from the barrel of Slocum's pistol.

He walked over to Ferro and climbed into the saddle. Then he reloaded his pistol and rode back into the valley.

Apaches screamed as they emerged from behind the buttes in bunches of three and four.

Gunfire erupted from rifles and painted bucks bit the dust everywhere he looked.

Slocum drew his rifle from its boot and rode into the fray. As he levered shell after shell into the chamber and started firing, the Apaches started dropping.

Finally, one warrior threw up his hands in surrender and rode toward Slocum.

Slocum held his fire.

"You are the one my braves told me about," he said in English. "I am Blue Wolf."

"Canby is dead," Slocum said. "The men here will fight you to the death."

"I know. I leave now. You have won."

Then Blue Wolf rode away, calling to his men. The Apaches melted into puffs of dust behind the buttes.

A silence settled over the valley.

The war was over.

The Apaches had carried off their dead, and the wagon was burned to a crisp, just a smoldering hulk in the middle of a valley that was peaceful once again.

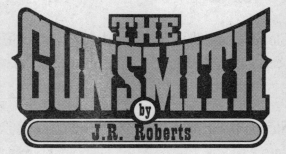